THE
METHUSELAH
GENE

MICHAEL S. MAURER

Also by Michael S. Maurer:
Water Colors (2003)
19 Stars of Indiana—Exceptional Hoosier Women (2009)
19 Stars of Indiana—Exceptional Hoosier Men (2010)
*10 Essential Principles of Entrepreneurship You Never Learned
    in School* (2012)
50 Crossword Puzzles with Playful Narrations (2015)
Cinderella Ball (2017)

Published by:
IBJ Book Publishing
One Monument Circle, Suite 300
Indianapolis, Indiana 46204
www.ibjbp.com

Published in both hardcover and trade paperback in 2021.

ISBN (Hardcover): 978-1-950143-14-6
First Edition
Library of Congress Control Number: 2021912910

ISBN (Trade Paperback): 978-1-950143-13-9
First Edition
Library of Congress Control Number: 2021912968

Printed in the United States of America

*This book is dedicated to my grandchildren,
Alexis, Tyler, Tessa, Cameron, Bella, Annie,
Sophie, Jonah and Eli.*

"We still are looking for someone who knows the secret of immortality. Only God is immortal; we are not."

—Elie Wiesel

PROLOGUE
2009

"Should I have taken Alex's advice and put off my own funeral?" Milt "Doc" Adams wondered as he leaned back in the pew at Second Pres. It was padded—cushy. Not like his church, Tab Presbyterian, with wooden benches, hard and smooth like the paddle his father took down from the wall next to the fireplace, as he used to say, "When necessary to make my point."

Dede, Doc's teenage granddaughter, had maneuvered his old red Cadillac into the church parking lot. Dede with a stretch could barely reach the pedals. Doc described her driving technique as tedious. They held hands as they entered the sanctuary after 11:00, only a few minutes late. Doc noticed the lingering glances from some of the men sitting in the aisles. Doc thought, "And why not? Dede's olive skin set off her hair—almost black and her eyes were cobalt blue like her father's." In Doc's younger days, Dede would have been referred to as "a looker."

Doc had dressed for the cool September morning in wool slacks, matching cable sweater knitted by his assistant, Mary Kellogg, and a favorite sport coat with elbow patches that had been replaced at least twice. No tie. At 77, funeral dress code compliance was not important to Doc. In fact, it never was. By the time he had set his hat and scarf on the seat next to him he was warm—too warm. Just before his eyes gave in to restful release, he whispered to no one in particular, "How does anyone get any praying done around here?"

Doc thought, "This is not a good day for a funeral. Last February in Chicago when we put Eddie Goldwald down—that was a day for a funeral." Eddie, Doc's college classmate at Duke, was a skilled poker player who played in a regular game for more than thirty years. His friends nicknamed him "Bret," after Bret Maverick, the TV gambler.

Eddie had succumbed to a benign brain tumor. Benign? It toyed with him. It robbed his energy, his mental acuity, and his personality, and when that was gone, it took his life. By the time he died, all he could manage was Old Maid.

Doc recalled when he and his wife, Janie, had powered their way up I-65 from Indianapolis to arrive at the Chicago cemetery a few minutes early, but when they opened the car doors all they saw were crosses. Janie had said, "Bret would never consent to be buried here." Doc had reminded her, "They wouldn't have wanted him anyway."

A tug at his sleeve interrupted his thoughts. Dede was under strict orders to take care of her grandfather. "Papa, you're grinning. This is not the place for it." Doc nodded to Dede and returned to his thoughts.

"We were lucky to have spotted that rabbi over the next hill. And was it cold! God whipped up the wind across Lake Michigan, added ice and sent it swirling across Lake Shore Drive just to remind the huddled mourners that the warmest soul in the neighborhood was Bret in the box they had just covered with Cook County's best soil." Doc felt a tremor. He sighed and shook his head.

Doc felt an elbow in his ribs. "You can't sleep at a funeral, Papa. For Pete's sake, we're in the third row."

Doc lifted his lids and tuned in to the proceedings. The officiant, a ruddy-faced post-teen in full regalia, including a gold vest and a cockeyed pointed hat, was reading a poorly chosen verse from the New Testament. Doc saw no connection between that passage and a funeral service or anything else. He was sure the boy in charge of this important ceremony had no idea and didn't seem to care who the deceased, Tina Morton, was and the full life she had led—the happiness and profound sadness she had experienced. He mused to himself, "He reminds me of the Jester." The Jester was a talented, even gifted, colleague who was often distracted—a good friend—but troubled. His lumpish demeanor prompted someone to brand him "the Jester," a less than complimentary sobriquet. Doc liked the Jester. Doc liked everyone.

Doc's eyes fluttered shut. Dede knew at a glance that Papa was not going to be roused. She just wouldn't mention this to her mother.

Doc mused, "Is there ever a good day for a funeral? What about today? No, not today—a crisp Indiana September day. Poor Mrs. Morton. It's days like this that I must ask myself, 'Did I make the right choice?'"

Afterward in his kitchen, Doc reached down and gave his granddaughter a hug, "Thank you guys for coming over and making me lunch, and thanks for driving me today, Dede. Appreciated but not needed. No idea why your mother insisted I give up my keys." Doc's daughter, Brenda, exchanged winks with Dede.

"Maybe, Papa, it was all those dents and scratches on your Cadillac."

"I'm not even eighty."

"You look good for your seventies. You still have a full head of hair. Mom wants to see you make ninety."

"I've stopped looking in the mirror. See these wrinkles?"

"I love your wrinkles, Papa. When you smile you are a beautiful man."

Doc straightened his frame in mock wonderment, a stature that had reached passed six feet—before Parkinson's began its vicious creep. "Tina Morton was over 100 when she gave up her car. She played golf and tennis in her nineties. They say last March she became the oldest Hoosier at 106."

Dede tossed her dark curls at her grandfather, "That explains why hardly anyone was at the funeral. All her friends are dead."

"You make a good point, Dede. Suppose you could live an extra 100 years. Would you choose to die rather than enter a future of uncertainty without friends or family?"

"I would love to live an extra 100 years if you lived them with me," Doc hugged his granddaughter.

"Tina did have a few friends left. Did you see Marty Colson, the guy who ran Rosenbaum Hospital for so many years? He was there. So was her attorney, my friend David Wexler. I spotted a reporter from the *Indianapolis Star* and some of Mrs. Morton's neighbors, including your boyfriend, Joe, with his mother. There were a few others."

Dede said, "His mother made him go." She added, "And that woman sitting in the back in the ugly green dress and flowered hat, she was the only one crying. I saw her come in. Did you see those high heels she was wearing? Polka dots! I'm not allowed to wear heels that high. Joe says he spotted her visiting the Morton house a number of times over the last few years. Maybe the ladies were having an affair. Some do that stuff, you know."

"Dede! You're sixteen years old," Doc said in mock surprise. "Brenda, where is your daughter getting her sex ed.?"

As if to prove her grandfather's point, Dede asked, "Papa, at what age do people stop thinking about sex?"

Brenda did not look up while she busied herself with grilled cheese sandwiches. Doc Adams couldn't mask his chuckle. "Dede, you'll have to ask an older man."

Dede continued unabashed, "Why were we there, Papa?"

"At the funeral? Tina Morton was Alex's mother. Alex was my closest friend."

"Joe told me Mrs. Morton's only son was a mad scientist who ran away years ago after murdering his wife. Joe said he might still be on the lam, but most people think he is so old he is probably dead. Is he your age, Papa? Joe said we haven't had a scandal like that since someone stuffed his girlfriend in a dresser drawer at the Claypool Hotel. Where would you run to, Papa? I think I would sail to Fiji. We read about that in social studies. The men wear skirts and the girls on the beach are topless. No matter to me. They wouldn't know whether I was coming or going."

Old Doc Adams raised an arm in protest. "Slow down, Dede, and eat your sandwich. Alex is not mad. Passionate, but not mad. He is a scientist ahead of his time. I would call him a "funeral postponement specialist." As for your boyfriend Joe, he is a great kid, but a bit prone to gossip, just like his mother."

Dede put down her grilled cheese, looked up at her grandfather and said, "How do you know that?"

"I was her pediatrician, and Joe's too. I don't want to discuss any of this, especially not today. If you want the scoop, ask your mother."

Dede fixed her eyes on her mother and grandfather. "I want to be a doctor like you, Papa. I'm going to take care of children. Mom, didn't you say it was in my DNA?"

"Yes dear, just like your sparkling blue eyes."

"Mom, you once said they were cobalt blue."

"Yes dear, they are." Brenda allowed her brown hair to show a natural touch of gray. She was not striking, like her daughter, but when she smiled, she was enticing. Brenda was soft-spoken and had always been that way. She bore a strong resemblance to her mother, who had passed away shortly after Dede was born.

Doc looked at Brenda, but spoke to Dede. "It's been a long morning, and I want to finish lunch and sit by the pond."

"I'll help you, Papa."

"Thanks Dede. Of course, I can make it myself."

"Of course, Papa."

Doc negotiated the winding path from his back porch down to the pond. He carefully avoided roots, rocks, and unfriendly terrain that needed the attention he had always intended to provide. He was pleased to accept the company and the support Dede offered, but he was not going to share that admission with anyone—not yet. He took measured steps, careful not to stumble or appear winded, observations that would surely be reported as soon as Dede returned to the kitchen.

In the spring the path was bordered by blazing yellow daffodils—Doc's favorite. A variety of summer blooms held sway until September, when somehow, they knew they were no match for the late blooming pink and white hostas that Brenda had planted just before Dede was born. In another month, more colors would emerge as the trees began to flaunt their foliage. Doc delighted in the change of seasons, but wondered how many more cycles he would be allowed before he was covered with earth, just like Eddie Goldwald. Funerals affected him that way.

The afternoon began to intrude upon the day, with the offering of a bright and warm sun. The trees along the path smelled of fruit. He had planted apple, cherry, and pear trees—or had them planted. The career of a pediatrician did not leave a lot of time to plant trees. The cherry trees never took root, but his apples flourished, and Brenda's apple crisp was a tasty indulgence with ice cream on a fall evening around the fire.

Doc thought, "If I weren't so damn tired, I would stop and pick one of those pears."

The path wound its way down to the pond—a noisy pond—crickets and frogs mostly. A careful listener could discern the sound of a woodpecker attacking one of the large pine trees in search of food or a place to nest. It reminded Doc of the tuning ritual of a symphonic orchestra. It was somehow soothing—nap-inducing. He and Dede both knew that. Just before the path played out at the pond's edge, it acquired a steeper grade. Many visitors found themselves ankle deep in water, unable to stem a slide of the last few feet. At the water's edge a wooden bridge stretched across the pond to a classic park bench given to Doc by a grateful family friend. Next to the bench a tree trunk protruded from the water about fifteen feet onto the bank—the only remnant of a giant oak felled by the ice storm of '76.

Dede tightened her grip on her grandfather's arm. "Are we walking around by the weeping willow or are we taking the bridge?"

"Let's take the bridge. It's the only apparatus that creaks louder than my bones."

Dede had heard the story of the Milton Adams Bridge from her mother, but her grandfather never mentioned it. According to Brenda, her father had often been invited to Rosenbaum Children's Hospital to assist with a diagnosis in spite of the fact that for a long time he was the youngest admitting pediatrician. One afternoon he was asked to examine a comatose four-year-old who had apparently hit her head after falling off a tricycle earlier that day. His colleague, Martin Colson, suspected a subdural hematoma that caused pooled blood to push on her brain. Colson was resourceful— enough so to ask for assistance when he needed it. In pre-med at Indiana University, he tested out of all of the first-year science courses, leaving just enough academic hours to cram in a separate degree in hospital administration. He was respected by his peers and the hospital staff— more important to him, he was liked.

On that afternoon, Doc Adams left a waiting room full of patients and dashed over to the hospital. "Thanks for coming, Milt. How is your little Brenda?"

"She's fine, thanks. Honored to get the call, Marty." Doc donned green hospital scrubs. Colson wore a blue suit and a red paisley tie. "Let's see if I can add anything."

Colson said, "By the way, this child is Bob Block's granddaughter, Marietta." Block was the largest developer of apartments in the Midwest and a supporter of many local charitable endeavors, including Junior Achievement, Girl Scouts, and Little League sports. More than one of Doc's patients had brought in a Block All Star Baseball trophy.

Doc's face had already begun to show some creases around his mouth, evidence of the smiles he shared with his patients throughout the day. It also bore a hint above the brow of his serious nature, which became more evident as he worked through the Block child's diagnosis.

While Doc examined the abrasions, the girl showed no reaction to the stimulus of his careful probing. Her eyes remained tightly shut when not forced open.

"Marty, no question her nervous system is shutting down. Her pupils are not responding to light and her breathing is irregular, but her abrasions are superficial, suggesting any intercranial damage would be highly unlikely. Besides, how bad can you hurt yourself by falling off a tricycle less than two feet off the ground? I wouldn't rule that out yet, though."

Colson put his hand on Doc's shoulder. "Milt, we both know the kid is comatose. I got that far without you. Since this condition has not begun to resolve itself, I am worried about long-term effects."

Doc barely looked up from his examination. He was gently flexing the girl's arms and legs. "Has the patient had any prior similar experiences?"

"Milt, up to this point the history is unremarkable."

"Marty, is she taking meds? Anything? Baby aspirin?"

"Nothing, Milt."

"Is she still producing urine?"

"Are you kidding? Take a look at that pad."

Let's get a drug screen on this urine STAT."

"What scripts is her mother on?"

"Her mother?"

Colson left the examining room and returned with a list of the drugs that the mother was taking. They looked at the list together—aspirin, Phenobarbital, a barbiturate prescribed for anxiety and sleeplessness, and Synthroid, a drug prescribed to boost an underactive thyroid.

"Marty, could the baby have swallowed some of her mother's Phenobarbital?"

The urine screen confirmed Doc Adams's suspicion. The girl recovered as soon as an infant dose of Naloxone was administered.

Colson telephoned Doc that evening. "Milt, the Block girl's vitals have improved, and her urine is clearer. Thanks, buddy, how did you figure this out?"

The day's interruption had caused Doc to run late. He had seen his last patient and he and Mary were closing shop. He said, "Instead of just asking 'What was the child's condition?' I asked 'Why? Why was she in this state?' I really didn't trust the subdural hematoma diagnosis, so I searched for another explanation."

"Did they teach you that at Duke?"

"No, my father was a physician. I think I picked up that technique at the dinner table."

Colson laughed over the phone. "My father owned a strip club. Someday I'll tell you what I picked up around our dinner table."

One evening later that week, when Doc was relaxing on his bench enjoying a fresh spring breeze, Bob Block hiked down to the pond to personally thank his friend for caring for his granddaughter. Block was no stranger to hiking. He had served as an army infantryman in World War II assigned to F Company in the Seventh Army, and was a participant in one of the most intense campaigns in history. His assignment was to help recapture several small villages, which had to be taken yard-by-yard in some of the fiercest fighting of the war. He always declined to discuss the number of enemy casualties he inflicted. When he returned home he decided that he had done enough to contribute to tearing down, even in a good cause, and he resolved to commit himself to the process of building, not only for his future, but for America's. He dubbed his newest project, "The Marietta."

Block's slacks showed a trace of mud from traversing the wet earth around the pond. Doc looked up, "Bob, how is little Marietta?"

"She is back to being impossible, thank God—and thank you, Dr. Adams."

"It's Milt."

"How can I ever thank you enough, Milt?"

"Thank Marty. It was a collaboration."

After a thoughtful silence, Bob looked up and declared, "I'm going to build you a bridge. Neither one of us will have to deal with muddy trousers again."

Three weeks later craftsmen from the Block Construction Co., a division of Block Industries, delivered and installed a bridge of fine maple, elegantly arched with hand-carved rails. It bore a plaque, "The Milton Adams Bridge, established 1968."

******

Old Doc Adams crossed the bridge on Dede's arm and settled down on the bench. "Shall I sit with you, Papa?"

"No, I'm expecting company."

"Hah, the only company that you can expect to see down here is the sandman." Dede swung her curls around as she bounded up the path. "Have a nice nap. I love you, Papa."

An hour later the old woman in the flowery hat did not slow to choose the safest course along the path. With her polka dot heels in hand she hastened down to the pond. She opted for the quiet dirt path by the willow tree rather than the creaky bridge and sat down on the oak tree trunk lying next to Doc's bench.

She began to disrobe. She let her jacket fall lightly to the ground. She set the flowery hat on the jacket. With a slight tug she lifted her wig and placed it carefully on the log next to the polka dot shoes. She stood in bare feet—now revealed as a man who looked to be in his forties, about five feet, six inches tall, wearing a ruffled green ankle-length dress, pink lipstick, and a broad smile. Doc turned toward the oak log and opened an eye. "Alex Morton, sorry about your mom. It's nice of you to visit. It's been almost thirty years."

PART ONE
PROGERIA

CHAPTER ONE
1972

The diagnosis was obvious and the prognosis—obvious, deadly obvious.

"Is he your patient, Marty?" Doc Adams asked. Doc had driven the two miles over to Rosenbaum Children's Hospital from his office on Central Avenue at the urging of his friend and colleague, Marty Colson. He often walked to the hospital—enjoying the 45-minute respite from his practice, already full after five years—but not today. He had already checked the chart and was gently thumping the two-and-a-half-year-old child when Colson entered the examining room. The chart described a healthy toddler, but one that had an arrested growth curve. Doc wrinkled his brow.

"No, Milt. Margo referred him in." Margo Thompson was one of three female practicing pediatricians with privileges at Rosenbaum. "Margo is a serious physician with a caring heart, perfect for a woman pioneering in pediatrics. She brings good paper to Rosenbaum. She's Johns Hopkins."

"Marty, I know Margo, and I agree. But get ready, Marty. This is the '70s. By the time we're in mid-career, there won't be any of us guys left in pediatrics."

Colson recently had been promoted to head of the Pediatric Department at Rosenbaum. Evaluation of personnel was one of his responsibilities. "Margo is competent but she's over her head on this one. Hell, I'm over my head on this one. There is a strange look to this boy. Thanks for lending a hand, Milt."

"I was planning to stop here later this afternoon anyway to round on a couple of yesterday's tonsillectomies."

Margo entered the examining room following a calming session with the baby's mother. She was a shade under five feet tall. Colson had described her hair and facial features in one word, "Cleopatra." Colson followed up on an earlier suggestion. "Margo, did you call the Jester?"

The Jester cultivated a wide range of specialties, including trauma. A resolute bachelor, he was known to be quirky, but occasionally inspirational in difficult or unusual situations. It was the Jester who had recognized Doc's telltale signs of early Parkinson's, including his failure to swing his left arm when he walked and the slight tremor that others had advised was a result of too much black coffee. The Jester's belly, a confession to his weakness for snacking, affected a rolling gait. One could always satisfy a sugar craving by sharing the half empty packets of chocolate-covered raisins and gummy bears he carried in his pockets. He was older than Doc by a few years and Colson by most of a decade but had just begun his practice when Doc arrived. The Jester owed his late start and a cigarette addiction to three years of Army service in Korea before he began medical school. Doc, in his fifth year in practice, knew him only as "the Jester." Colson had forgotten the Jester's given name years ago. It was Ralph Jessup.

"No, Dr. Adams, I did not phone the Jester." Margo was not in the Jester fan club. She had overcome adversity to earn admission to medical school and later garnered a coveted position at Johns Hopkins. She had little respect for what she observed was the Jester's whimsical attitude toward practicing medicine. Where Margo saw whimsy, Doc sensed a troubled soul.

Marty turned, looking for comfort, "I'm named head of this department for less than six months and in comes an impossible diagnosis."

Doc Adams gently tapped the boy on both sides just below the neck. "Margo, please order an x-ray of this boy's collarbone."

"Yes, Marty, this diagnosis is difficult because it is a condition I suspect none of us has observed. I read about it in medical school. One of my Dad's textbooks even had a photograph. If you had seen that picture, you never would have forgotten it. The diagnosis would have been as obvious to you as it is to me."

Doc raised the toddler's left foot. His toes were folded inward. When Doc held the boy's ankle and slowly straightened the big toe, the child yanked his foot from the doctor's grasp and screamed.

"What's the boy's name?"

"Jimmy, Jimmy Higgins."

"Now, Jimmy, we are not going to hurt you." Jimmy was not convinced. "Margo, please ask Jimmy's mother to join us."

Deborah Higgins could hear her son's screams of mortal terror from the waiting room. She needed no further prompting to dash down the hall. Margo turned to her patient's mother, "Please help us calm Jimmy." A mother's embrace, soothing words and light taps on the boy's back settled him down. Mrs. Higgins knew to avoid the top of her son's chest.

"What's the matter with Jimmy? At his last checkup six months ago Dr. Thompson said he was doing fine, but he is not growing, and he stopped teething." Mrs. Higgins closed her eyes and clasped the fingers of her right hand around the cross that hung from her delicate silver necklace. When she reopened her eyes, she managed a weak smile. "My brother told me he was dentally retarded."

Doc did not look up from carefully flexing the boy's limbs. They were less than fluid. "Mrs. Higgins, in a way your brother is correct, but I am afraid it is more serious than that. Have you noticed a slight change in your son's skin tone?"

"Yes, and his hair used to be so thick like his father's. What happened to his eyebrows?"

"Mrs. Higgins, we have completed our examination. Please take Jimmy and wait for Dr. Thompson in her office. She will join you shortly."

When the door closed, Doc addressed his colleagues. "Marty, the x-ray of his collarbone will show bone disintegration. Dr. Thompson, did you notice the prominent vein structure in the scalp and the child's facial appearance, particularly the eyes?" Doc continued without waiting for an answer. "Your patient, Jimmy Higgins, has a genetic mutation of unknown etiology that grossly accelerates the aging process. It turns children into old people. It is called progeria."

Dr. Thompson shuddered. "For land's sake. There was a case at Hopkins. I never saw the baby, though." She hadn't bargained for this. "What are we to do?"

"This condition goes back at least a half-century, and as far as I know, there is no cure. Jimmy will age before our eyes and will surely not survive his teenage years. He will probably suffer from early onset in childhood of accelerated progressive arteriosclerosis and die of a myocardial infarction or stroke, like many people in their late eighties. The only treatment options we have are supportive care and therapies directed toward the complications arising from the disease."

Doc fought back tears. He continued. "Margo, Jimmy should see a specialist, but since he is probably the only progeria sufferer within 500 miles, we are not going to find an expert in Indy. I would refer Jimmy upstairs to Alex Morton. I have not met Dr. Morton, but I know he is a newly minted pediatric oncologist who generally sees tumors, bone cancer, and blood diseases. Jimmy does not have cancer, but Dr. Morton is heralded as a resourceful researcher with experience in the lab."

Colson added, "He was highly recommended to the hospital. According to Dr. Bennett, his mentor at MD Anderson, he has a complex understanding of molecular and cellular biology and other research in the field, including genetics. He is compact, but what a dynamo. We were lucky to add him to our staff. I think the only reason we landed him was because his wife has family nearby."

Thompson nodded her head. "That's right, Marty. Her father, Logan Howell, owns an automobile auction."

"Not just an automobile auction, Margo. Howell on the Block is one of the largest chains of auto auctions in the world. He runs millions of cars through his auctions and takes a piece of every one. If he is not the richest guy in Indiana, he will be soon."

Doc said, "Have you solicited him for a gift?"

"He's on my list. He's on everyone's list."

"You can make money in that business?" Doc was neither aware of nor concerned about the super wealthy.

"You can make money at anything if you're the best." Colson replied. "I read an article in the *Wall Street Journal* about an airport shoe-shine boy who became a millionaire. His customers walked in not only wearing shoes for him to shine, they walked in *with* shoes. He developed such a following that he hired employees who he trained to his level of excellence."

Doc packed his bag, "I've got to get back to the office. My pager is exploding."

Colson paced the floor. "We're all going to have to shine shoes around here to pay for what I committed to Alex Morton. I promised him we would develop Rosenbaum into a center of excellence in pediatric oncology within ten years."

"Did he believe you?"

"He believed me, all right. He even moved his mother and father to Indy. His father took a job as chief customer officer with Howell on the Block."

As Doc left the examining room he turned back and said, "Marty, you may have over-promised. If Dr. Morton believed that, maybe he is not as smart as you think."

CHAPTER TWO

Doc Adams' office was in an old one-story home at 38th Street and Maple Avenue, a formerly stately neighborhood gracefully surrendering its charm. Rosenbaum Children's Hospital was within a five minute drive. Its board had not succumbed to the pressure to relocate nearer to the newer suburban neighborhoods several miles north, where most of its doctors resided, but there was always talk in the doctor's lounge of "new-building fund-raising." Doc was pleased to serve the walk-in trade, but most of his patients were from the suburbs and journeyed twenty minutes or more with their moms to see the exceptional young pediatrician. Within five years of opening, his practice and waiting room were full. He capped his suburban practice but continued to accept new patients from the neighborhood.

The day after Doc diagnosed the Higgins boy, his nurse tapped him on the shoulder. "There is a call for you, Dr. Adams, from a doctor at Rosenbaum, a Dr. Morton."

"Mary, I'll have to call him back. We are knee-deep in measles, shots, and earaches. See if I can catch him around five."

"Have you seen your waiting room? You'll never get out of here by five," Mary shrugged. "Neither will I."

It was after six when the two doctors connected. "Dr. Adams, this is Alex Morton. Thanks for the referral of the Higgins boy. I'm not sure what I can do for the poor kid, but I'll give it a go. I've read the progeria literature. That's not a big chore. There is no disease-modifying therapy. I've located three children facing this challenge. The closest one is in Iowa. No one can add much.

One is sixteen years old. That's encouraging. The question is, how did she get there when most of the kids are dying in their early teens? Hey, I'm going on and on. Our wives have met. How about dinner together this week where I can thank you in person for the confidence you have shown in me. I'll ask Betsy to call your wife."

The following Monday night, Mary fielded another call for Dr. Adams. The Adams office sported no intercom facility. Mary just hollered down the hall. "Your wife is on the phone." Family policy and good sense dictated that Doc took those calls—STAT.

"Yes, Janie?"

"Be home by 6:00. We are going out with the Mortons tonight."

The wives chose Foxy's in Broad Ripple, an Indianapolis neighborhood enjoying a renaissance after a near total collapse more than ten years before at the hands of a regional mall. Foxy's suited the women perfectly—diet-conscious salads with small pasta portions. The guys settled on pasta—larger portions. Betsy and Janie were friends from Betsy's first telephone call. They were already playing tennis, shopping and conspiring to make sure their husbands shared their enthusiasm. Janie was normally reserved—not cliquey, but cautious. Betsy overcame that hesitancy with a bear hug at their first meeting. Janie laughed with Betsy, who was quick with an off-color comment. Some of Janie's friends said Betsy had a "mouth." Janie loved that.

Doc was five years older than Alex. In addition, he had enjoyed a few years of private practice while Alex earned his fellowship in pediatric oncology. Doc gained insight listening to his father, a competent practitioner and a caring mentor. Alex, whose father was an automobile mechanic, was street-smart in every sense of the word.

Alex picked up the check. "I just want to say thanks one more time for the Higgins referral. When I was at MD Anderson ..." Betsy cut in, "Name dropper." "Sorry, anyway, I participated in basic cell research. Maybe I can prolong Jimmy's life." Alex shook his head and paused in silence as he looked at each person around the table. "Progeria's effect on longevity is probably due to a genetic mutation. The theory is fascinating and, I apologize if I sound like a megalomanic, but studying progeria at the cellular level could yield secrets to aging and to life itself."

CHAPTER THREE

"Everything is white. Everything about it is white," sobbed Margo Thompson, as she shared her first impression of Northbridge College in Ashland, Wisconsin, with her mother over the telephone. "Snow, snow, snow everywhere." But it's not just the weather. There are 4,000 kids here, and none of them look like me. Thompson had taken the bus from her home in segregated Pineville on the north bank of the Red River in Rapides Parish, Louisiana. "Momma, the bus took two days to get here and it seemed every hour it got colder and whiter. It was like a journey to the Twilight Zone."

In the 1960s, young women like Margo Thompson could dream. Thompson knew that advancement and achievement on a broad scale was possible for African Americans, and she came north to compete for her share of America.

"Momma, I miss y'all, and I don't know why, but I miss Pineville. I am going to stick it out. Tell that to Daddy." Thompson's father was an assistant college professor who taught biology at nearby Louisiana State University-Alexandria on the other side of Red River. Thompson's mother, Bertha Lou, was one of nine children. She was known as "Big Bertha,"—all five feet of her. Her job title at George's General Store was "head cashier." No one doubted who ran the store. On weekends, she volunteered at the city library. The librarian, Wendy Brown, encouraged her to check out children's books for her daughter. Margo Thompson became an avid reader.

Although the civil rights movement had begun and the South was beginning to feel the trauma of integration in the hot spots of Alabama and Mississippi, there was little immediate effect on the quiet and "polite" bigotry in Rapides Parish.

As a young girl, Thompson had a severe stutter that persisted in first and second grades. She was branded "T-T-T-T-Thompson" and teased in the schoolyard. There was only one child psychologist who worked with language problems in Alexandria and three speech pathologists with Children's Hospital in Baton Rouge, more than 100 miles southeast of Pineville. All were white and refused to provide care to African Americans. Big Bertha contacted the NAACP, which threatened a lawsuit. In response, speech therapy services were offered by Louisiana Children's Hospital through Dr. Cameron Bryan, on the condition that Thompson receive therapy only after hours and that she agree to not occupy the patient lounge or use the facilities in the doctor's office. Big Bertha objected, but agreed when informed that delays could affect the effectiveness of her daughter's care.

Within three weeks, Dr. Bryan waived the fees for her precocious seven-year-old patient and new friend. She used a metronome to slow and regulate Thompson's speech cadence, gradually speeding up the pace of her delivery. Dr. Bryan taught Thompson to sing the Lord's Prayer. They sang together, "Give us *this* day our daily *bread*." After two months of weekly therapy sessions, her Ts and Bs were perfect. When each session ended, Thompson was tasked to carefully recite the following words, "metronome, tick, tick, tick." Dr. Bryan cautioned Margo, "Remember, coordinate your communication cadence with your thought processes. If you become flustered or get ahead of yourself, stop and say our magic words, 'metronome, tick, tick, tick.'"

As they began their third month together, Dr. Bryan brought a list of 250 words that often appeared on the SAT college entrance exam. Bryan declared to her prodigy, "Margo, some homework. While we are learning to speak words let's also learn what they mean. Each week memorize the meanings of ten words from this list and speak each one to me in a sentence."

Three months later Margo announced, "Mama insists that I do not need any additional work. When I began therapy sessions with you my speech was abysmal. I had to endure malicious taunts from my classmates which served to exacerbate my problem. I am not eloquent but these sessions with you have bolstered my confidence. You have rescued me. I love you, Dr. Bryan."

Cameron Bryan dabbed at her eyes and hugged her little patient. "Margo, you have changed my life. You have taught me something about myself. It is I who owe you a thank you. I love you Margo." The adversity Margo experienced as a young child and the kindness shown by Dr. Bryan guided her decisions as she dedicated her life to helping others.

Thompson earned a perfect high school academic record and was salutatorian of her graduating class. She was recruited by a number of schools. Thompson chose Northbridge College on the basis of location—far away from Pineville. The school offered her a full ride.

At Northbridge, Thompson selected a double major in chemistry and biology. In her first chemistry class, the professor decreed that each day the last two people to finish the exercises were responsible for cleaning up the lab. Thompson and her lab partner, George Taylor, also an African American, always ended up with the mop and the broom. They were afraid that a misstep would blow up the entire lab, so they rechecked each step in their experiments. It seemed to Thompson that white students knew exactly what steps to perform in the lab. Upon inquiry, it became apparent that her classmates were better prepared from their high school chemistry classes. She concluded that Louisiana clung to the doctrine of "separate but equal" and in Louisiana "separate but equal" was anything but equal in the chemistry laboratory.

One day three weeks after leaving the lab "broom clean," Thompson went two doors down the hall to her professor's office. "Dr. Watson, I love chemistry but I need a little boost until I feel more confident with the experiments."

Watson replied, "Miss Thompson, meet me every day about 45 minutes before class. That should be the solution." Watson laughed at his own pun. Thompson began making A's on all of her exams. She excelled in chemistry and all of her subjects.

Thompson's roommate, Ingrid Lungren, was Scandinavian. Almost six feet tall, she was a foot taller than Thompson. She complained, "I'm sick of this dorm food, so I'm going home this weekend. How about joining me? Maybe Saturday you can help me prepare for next week's biology exam. I'd like you to meet my mom and dad."

"Thank you, Ingrid. That's mighty kind."

"Super, we can take the bus to Green Bay after class on Friday."

Thompson was a regular guest of the Lungrens' throughout the year. Many of the family were often in attendance, including Ingrid's three young nieces, one of whom admired her "chocolate suntan." It was an awkward moment, but the family welcomed Margo in a loving embrace.

After three years in college, Thompson was accepted into the Indiana University School of Medicine in Indianapolis, not as snowy and a little closer to home—and not quite so white. Leaving Wisconsinites behind, she encountered a new breed, Hoosiers. Thompson excelled in medical school and chose to stay in Indiana for her internship. After a residency in pediatric medicine at Washington University in St. Louis, Thompson secured her first job, a prestigious research-oriented faculty position in the Division of Pediatric Diseases at the Johns Hopkins University School of Medicine. At Hopkins she taught infectious diseases. After two years, she was recruited back to Indiana to join the practice of colleagues with whom she had interned. Rosenbaum granted her admitting privileges on the day she arrived.

Before returning to begin her practice in Indiana, Thompson spent five days in Pineville saying farewell to her family and marrying her old lab partner, George Taylor, who discovered he was better suited for law than medicine. Ingrid Lungren served as her maid of honor. Dr. Cameron Bryan was an honored guest.

There was no trace of "T-T-T-T-Thompson" in the self-assured, attractive physician at Rosenbaum Children's Hospital. At an all-staff meeting soon after she arrived, Marty Colson closed his introduction with, "A girl of seventeen, Margo followed her dreams across the United States, from the deep South to our country's heartland. Her quest for education and high achievement led her to Indiana. Margo's determination to improve the health and well-being of her fellow Hoosiers is evident. She has already earned our respect and admiration. Her ideals and dedication set a standard to which we should all aspire."

CHAPTER FOUR

Betsy Howell arrived on the campus of Indiana University in the fall of 1956, just before her 18th birthday. Like many coeds, she burst with excitement and promise. She was only slightly intimidated by the large collegiate population and the pressure to make grades and join one of the preferred sorority houses.

Her high school transcript was above the median benchmark for the entering class, and her list of high school clubs, organizations, and activities ran for pages. Her yearbook feature lauded her singing, dancing, and acting skills. Her grade point average could have been higher had she not opted to enjoy everything the Carmel High School curriculum afforded, including a lively social life. She was slender yet shapely—an attractive teen. The dimples she inherited from her mother, an avid athlete from Montreal, who had been a forward on her high school soccer team. Her daring—that was from her father, Logan, whose entrepreneurial skills were polished in the rough street wars of the automobile industry.

The boys liked her. She liked them too. She could kiss for hours. Like many of the girls her age, she tried sex—twice. The first time it happened quite suddenly on the couch in her home after the family went to sleep. She said to herself, "If that's it, I must be missing something." She tried it again with the same high school baseball player. She confided to her girlfriends at a slumber party, "I am not enthralled with the whole thing. What is the fuss about?"

Betsy joined the Pi Gamma Phi sorority house and grades ceased to be a priority. Many of her friends in Pi Phi shared her enthusiasms and curiosity. One evening eight sisters decided to go to the Timber Tavern, a local bar and dance hall. They had purchased fake IDs from Jolten Joe at the Acacia house. The Pi Phis referred to him as JJ. None of the girls knew his real name. Many suspected he was more than one guy, rather a profitable enterprise passed down among the Acacias for more than a decade. Betsy's new ID, an Indiana driver's license, read "Paula Richfield." She memorized the birthday, September 4, 1935. They donned pink T-shirts that read "Pi Phis on Phire." At the last minute they opted to go commando—no underwear. On Betsy, the costume change was complimentary—sexually obvious but not obnoxious. The outfits included short white skirts and red beanies. Betsy and her sorority sister, Sally Henry, were the only two non-blondes in the group. Betsy was talented, but Sally was the best of the dancing Pi Phis. She had jet black hair, a sultry look, and a body many of the guys described as fearsome.

One evening, Sally encouraged patrons—ladies and men—to form a circle around her. As she twirled, her jet-black hair was noticeable in more than one place. Police were called and by order of their authority, the Timber Tavern was closed. After a week of negotiation with university authorities and city hall, the closure order was rescinded. Under its terms, Sally had to wear underwear. Guys reported she wore a thong. There was no mention of costume requirements for the rest of the Pi Phis on Phire. Sally Henry acquired the nickname "Sally No Pants Henry." She dated constantly. The "Phires" became a semi-regular feature at Timber Tavern on Thursday nights.

During her second semester at IU, Betsy met Tim, a senior with a convertible and long blond hair, not hippy long, but hip. He was president of his fraternity, Phi Sigma Kappa. At six foot one, he was a solid athlete, just below varsity team level, an intramural star in a number of sports. It didn't take long for Tim to change Betsy's outlook on "making love," as she began to call it. Tim answered all those journalism questions. He knew where, when, and how. Betsy longed all week for weekends in bed with Tim. The couple knew the location of every motel in Bloomington.

Around four on a Friday afternoon in May, Betsy's phone rang. She was expecting the call. "Betsy." It was Tim. "I'll pick you up around six thirty. I got us a place at the Harvest House on Walnut Street."

"That's great, Tim. That's exciting."

Tim continued, "By the way, do you mind if I ask Bailey to join us? He's my fraternity brother. You met him at Tulagi the other day, the one from Vincennes. He just wants to have a few drinks and then he'll leave. I'm bringing tequila."

Betsy said, "Last month a bunch of us walked over to El Verde for dinner. We ended up at the bar drinking margaritas. We had to carry Sally back to the sorority house. Bring salt." She hesitated, "But I'm uncomfortable with having anybody in the same motel room with us."

Tim was ready with a reply, "He won't bother us, and he'll leave after we have a few drinks. I'll make sure of that."

Tim, Bailey, and Betsy shared funny stories around a table in their Harvest House motel room while smoking Marlboros and downing shots of tequila from the bathroom glasses. Betsy thought Bailey was a little goofy looking, with his gap-toothed smile and slicked-back red hair. He talked kinda funny too, in a southern Indiana twang. When Betsy asked him if he wanted more ice, he said, "Don't make me no difference." She thought that was hilarious. The three of them laughed. Tim noticed that Betsy held onto the table to keep from falling off her chair. She reached under the table for Tim's thigh and said, "I feel tingly all over. Oh, Tim, I want you so."

After a few more shots, Betsy felt fuzzy. Tim reached over as she rose, and they enjoyed a long, lingering embrace. Betsy whispered, "Tell Bailey to leave, please." Tim guided Betsy to the king bed on the other side of the room and whispered back, "He's not going to see anything in this dim light. Let him sit there and drink his shots." Betsy took one more shot and attempted to undress under the covers just to make sure. "Please help me, Tim." They both tried to be very quiet. Just as Tim entered her, she felt the presence of another body on her left side. Bailey, also naked, had slipped under the covers and was squeezing Betsy's right breast. Tim paid no attention. Betsy reached up and pushed Bailey's arm away. He caught her arm and placed her hand between his legs. Bailey went back to Betsy's breast gently squeezing and pulling on her nipple. Tim kept about his business. Betsy, with Tim inside her and her hand on Bailey's erect penis, was unleashed. She felt a thrill she had never experienced. She said to herself, "Bailey's thing is huge. I can't even get my hand around it." She gripped it tighter and in a matter of moments she felt a rumble deep within her. Her leg began to shake. A sound emanated from her lips, a sound Betsy had never heard before, and then again louder and deeper as she reached her ultimate ecstasy. Tim expended himself fully and rolled out of bed.

Bailey was on her and in her before she could think about what was happening next. She thought, "He really is large." She whispered, "Please, you shouldn't." She moaned, "Bailey you fill me completely." And in a voice only she could hear, she murmured, "Don't come." Bailey couldn't hold back. Neither could Betsy.

She struggled to sit up and said, "Tim, how about a drink of water?"

Tim said, "Try this and handed her the tequila bottle from which she took a swig."

She said with more than a little embarrassment, "I really need to get back to the sorority house." Tim stood before her naked and pleaded, "Betsy, just once more, we always do it at least twice." She smiled her consent and he climbed in and held her as his manhood returned, so did her lust. This time she made no pretense about her modesty. Bailey was at her side sucking one breast and pinching the other nipple. Betsy's hand sought out Bailey's big toy and moved her hand up and down his entire length. Betsy hoped it would never end. When Tim was finished, Betsy turned over on her stomach to catch her breath and her world went dark. Both boys rose from the bed.

A few minutes later Bailey said, "I'm plumb tuckered out, but I reckon I can plow this field one more time." With a nod of approval from Tim, he dived back in bed. He slipped his arm under Betsy and flipped her over like a dead flounder.

Betsy awoke and pleaded, "No, Bailey, I can't anymore." Bailey paid no attention. He raised Betsy's legs, forced them apart with both knees and invaded her. "No, Bailey, please, no." She felt no ecstasy, only pain. Bailey leaned into her breast and licked her nipple. He guided it into the space between his front teeth and closed his mouth. Betsy screamed. She pleaded, "Tim, please tell him to stop." Bailey bit her other nipple. Betsy reached her hands to push Bailey off, but he grabbed both wrists. His knees pinned her legs to the bed. Bailey laughed and slowed his pace to fierce thrusts. Betsy, unable to move, looked up and saw Tim grinning at the scene. Bailey laughed again enjoying his control—his mastery. When he finished, he slapped her across the face.

Betsy arose from the bed, put on her clothes and walked out the door. No tears were shed. As she walked back to her sorority house, she said to herself, "No more tequila. No more Tim. And no more sex." And then she met Alex.

CHAPTER FIVE

Alex grew up in West Mifflin, a suburb of Pittsburgh. It was not a suburb for the country club set like Squirrel Hill, but a neighborhood that boasted a proud steel worker tradition, a neighborhood of solid jobs and unbroken families.

Alex worked after school and on weekends with his father, Kevin, at Morton Mechanics, Inc., the family auto-repair garage. He delighted in bending over the fender of a Ford or Chrysler with his father to diagnose and treat sick oil pumps, carburetors, and generators. At the shop, Alex referred to his father as "Kevin." At home it was "Dad," spoken with admiration and respect. His grades in high school were not remarkable, mainly Bs with a smattering of As and the occasional C. It was the As that were spectacular: physics, chemistry, biology, and advanced algebra. He learned the material and could knead it like fresh dough. His private discussions with instructors demonstrated an understanding and facility with the subjects often beyond their comprehension. His biology teacher, Mrs. Wellbrook, implored him to look beyond the boundaries of the West Mifflin family garage and embrace the sciences to find his life's work.

Alex was a good-natured friend who enjoyed hanging with high school buddies, of which he had many. His easygoing personality masked a keen competitive spirit, which dissolved once in a while into flashes of temper. He excelled in team sports, especially football, until age 11, when he noticed that his classmates were much bigger.

At sixteen, when he could afford it, he joined friends on ski trips to nearby Laurel Highlands. His unfailing balance and aggressive style won him medals in downhill racing. In high school, he opted out of football and joined the Titans wrestling team, where he could contest boys his own weight. By his junior year that weight was 138 pounds of muscle spread over his still growing five-foot, four-inch frame.

In a heated match with rivals from Rankin High School, his opponent head-butted him just above his ear, a clear violation of the rules. Alex disregarded the illegal blow and brought his opponent to the floor with his reliable single-leg pickup. At the beginning of the next period, when both players were standing, his opponent head-butted him once more. Alex complained to the referee, who responded, "Don't be a baby. We are here to wrestle, not bellyache." Encouraged, his opponent head-butted him yet again. Alex put his hand behind his opponent's neck and held it securely while he smashed his head across the bridge of his opponent's nose. The crack could be heard in the chemistry lab across the hall. The boy reached his hands up to his nose in reaction to the pain. Alex kneed him in the groin and the boy fell in a bleeding groaning clump.

Alex leaned down to his opponent and whispered, "Would you like to get up and finish the match?"

The referee blew his whistle and declared, "This bout is over." He blew his whistle again, but he had lost control to boos from the home fans in the bleachers and cheers from the Titans wrestling team. The referee attempted to raise the Rankin boy's arm in victory, but he was still on the floor. The referee stepped around the Rankin coach and his propped-up wrestler to approach the scorer's table. He flipped on the PA system and announced to the assemblage, "I hereby cancel the remainder of this match and award victory to the Rankin Tigers based upon the severe, unsportsmanlike behavior of the Titans team!" No one heard what else the referee said over the roar from the Titans team and its coaches. Alex's teammates screamed and yelled and applauded as they filed down to the visitors' locker room.

The next morning, administrative assistant Sophie Garten made her announcements over the loudspeaker during the homeroom period:

"Good morning, students, and welcome to another wonderful day at West Mifflin Central High. Remember, tryouts for the 1955 Junior Spectacular begin on Thursday. Please contact Mrs. Shoemaker in room 210 if you would like a slot on the agenda. The French Club will meet after school today in the cafeteria. Congratulations to our girls' cross-country team for extending its fall winning streak to five. Coach Vallieu and our Titans wrestling team lost to the Rankin Tigers last night by forfeit."

Alex's class erupted in applause. The story had gotten around. Later that day Alex learned of his suspension from the team for the remainder of the season on the order of the Pennsylvania State High School Athletic Commission.

On Saturday Kevin and Alex paused for lunch at the shop. Alex said, "Dad, I need to talk with you. I need some advice. It's about what happened at the wrestling meet and about Mimsy Hammerman."

"Girl trouble, huh. Well ..."

"No Dad. No girl trouble. Just listen. The kid from Rankin, I broke his nose. I'm sure I broke his nose. I heard it crack. I feel awful. I should never have lost my temper."

"Alex, I have always counseled you to defend yourself, but in the controlled environment of a high school wrestling meet you made a mistake."

"I know Dad, I could have beaten the guy fair and square."

"Alex, that's irrelevant. Play by the rules whether you could win or not."

"You are right, Dad. What do I do now? Oh, and the matter of Mimsy Hammerman. She is a senior and she barely even says hello to me in the hall. Did I tell you she was the junior prom queen last year? Now, because of the wrestling notoriety her friends have told me that she wants to go out with me. I'd give anything for a date with her, but I don't deserve it based upon my disgusting behavior. I need some advice."

"First, ask Coach Vallieu to provide you the name of the Rankin boy. We'll find the address and you can apologize to him in person. I'll go with you. While we're doing all that, don't waste another moment. Call the Hammerman girl, Mimsy, right? And get that date before she changes her mind."

Alex declined to return to the wrestling team his senior year, opting to spend his afternoons as an unpaid research assistant and gofer at Penn Bio, Inc., an independent drug testing facility. He told Coach Vallieu, "I am not a fighter. I want to be a healer."

Based on teacher recommendations, decent grades, and excellent achievement tests, particularly in math, Alex was offered five college scholarships. He spurned an offer from the University of Pittsburgh and seized the opportunity to break from the comfort of his hometown routine. He accepted a partial scholarship from Indiana University, where he enrolled in a pre-med program majoring in zoology.

During his freshman year in Bloomington, Indiana, he rarely left the library. His grades were straight As. That summer he helped manage his father's garage. On his last day as a mechanic, he hugged his father and said, "I will always miss working with you, Dad."

CHAPTER SIX

In September of his sophomore year at IU, Alex was studying for a zoology quiz when two friends barged into his dorm room and chucked his textbook across the room. "We're walking over to the Timber Tavern for a beer. The Pi Phis on Phire are dancing tonight. We'll only stay for an hour. You can study when you get back." When Alex saw Betsy, he felt like Tony when he saw Maria in Broadway's new hit, *West Side Story*. He was enchanted by her eyes—hazel with flecks of blue. He wished he had taken the time to shave and comb his hair. He was sure the line, "You are beautiful," would never work. He approached Betsy and said, "You are beautiful." They talked and danced. At seven a.m. the next day he called her for a date. They saw no one else for the rest of the year.

Betsy became the second dancer to drop out of the Pi Phis on Phire. "Sally No Pants" did not return to the sorority house for her sophomore year. It was said she was living in one of the married housing units. Patrons still asked about her.

For the first two months of their relationship, Betsy and Alex spent hours in each other's arms kissing and petting. Finally, one night Betsy sat up in the backseat of her new Oldsmobile and said, "Alex, you make me so excited, I want to make love with you."

Alex was silent. He stuttered, "Not tonight, Betsy. He went silent once again. Her eyes searched for a clue. Alex said, "I, um, I'm a virgin."

Betsy giggled, "Oh, Alex, we'll take care of that soon."

The next day, Betsy found Alex in Hyatt Hall as he exited his chemistry class.

Alex said, "What a nice surprise to see you between classes."

"Between classes? Your school day is over, Buster!"

Alex did not argue. They walked holding hands to Betsy's car. When he noticed a picnic basket and a blanket in the backseat, he said, "I'm supposed to be in the lab this afternoon to complete an experiment that is due tomorrow."

"Tell you what, Alex. I'll help you with an experiment. We'll write it up together, and you can turn it in tomorrow." Betsy was flushed. She hadn't had sex for six months. Before they left for the summer break, "Sally No Pants" had treated the Phires to vibrators she purchased from the adult bookstore on Pearl Street. Betsy was too embarrassed to remove hers from the box. Alex knew the experiment Betsy had in mind and said to himself, "I hope I don't botch this."

After half an hour, Betsy pulled through the gates of Brown County State Park and parked in the lot nearest the trails. Alex carried the picnic basket. Betsy carried her blanket, a soft cotton adorned with flower buds in pastel shades. After 100 yards and two left turns, they found a secluded clearing. It was 11:00 a.m. on a Tuesday, a quiet time in the park. As Betsy leaned over to lay out the blanket, the mid-morning sun embraced her auburn hair with its golden highlights. Alex breathed those first few words once again. "You are beautiful."

Betsy pretended not to notice. She said, "Alex, you want something to eat?"

"Are you kidding me?" He tackled her, and they both went down in a passionate embrace. Betsy lifted her skirt and removed her panties. She held Alex's hand and guided it up and down her thighs and into new territory.

Betsy said, "We have a lot of basic training ahead of us this morning. Drop your jeans, Alex." He took off his pants and underwear—shirt too. "Now, I'm going to lie here with my legs wide apart and my knees slightly bent. You lie on me with your legs kinda together. Don't worry, I'm going to help you here." She inserted him as she moved her hips upward. Alex climaxed in the same moment.

He said out loud, "Oh, shit. I botched it."

Betsy was amused, "Yep, but I'll give you another chance. They lay back on the blanket. Alex fixed his cobalt blue eyes on Betsy and said, "I love you."

Betsy laughed, "Are you sure it's not this great sex?"

Betsy sighed on their third try, as she felt the rumble of an orgasm possess her body.

Betsy closed her eyes. "I hear crickets. Do you hear that chirping? I thought crickets only chirped in the evening."

Alex traced the fingers of his hand across Betsy's flat stomach up to and around her breast. "I learned on a Boy Scout overnight hike that only male crickets chirp and often in celebration of successful mating."

Alex, can you chirp? Chirp for me. Alex, come on, chirp!"

Alex couldn't chirp, but he knew the next best thing. Betsy thought, "This guy is a fast learner." Afterward Betsy reached into the picnic basket and offered Alex a sandwich. "Egg salad?"

"Ugh, I hate egg salad."

Betsy winked at her new lover, "OK, other than that, how's the morning going for you, Alex?"

By winter break Alex was a guest of the Howell family in Carmel, a wealthy suburb just north of Indianapolis. He was an instant hit with Betsy's father, Logan, her mother, Emily, and her two younger brothers. Each morning between 3:00 and 4:00 a.m. Betsy slipped down the hall to the guest bedroom and into Alex's waiting arms. They weren't fooling anybody. By his junior year the romance was all-consuming. His grades slipped—he pulled a B in advanced calculus.

CHAPTER SEVEN

During their senior year at IU, Betsy and Alex often frequented Tulagi, a hangout where they could flash their fake IDs to have a beer and a stromboli. Alex was on a tight budget. Betsy was not. She preferred sushi and sirloin, but she respected Alex's discipline and rarely pressed for more elegant fare.

Tulagi was established in 1948 by Joseph Berkey, whose son, Marine Corporal Hiram Berkey of Company B, First Raider Batallion, perished in 1942 on the Island of Tulagi in the Solomon Islands. New patrons of Tulagi were startled by entire tables raising their mugs in unison and shouting, "To Hiram!" A photograph of Hiram hung in the bar entryway beside a depiction of the battle for the Solomon Islands. They soon learned that everyone who toasted Hiram received a 5 percent discount on the tab.

One evening at a table across the room, Alex noticed four guys staring in his direction and laughing. He said to Betsy, "Do you know those people?"

She looked up without turning her head and said, "I know the one with the red hair. His name is Bailey."

"Why is he laughing at us?" Alex asked.

Betsy barely spoke the words, "When I was a freshman, he raped me." The tears that she had held for three years burst forth in waves and sobs. Alex shooed the waitress away when she approached the table to offer assistance.

Alex moved from across the table to Betsy's side and whispered, "Betsy, you go on home. I know you have a psych exam tomorrow.

I'm going to sit here and nurse my beer. I love you, Betsy." She wiped her tears with a paper napkin and rose. She stared straight ahead as she bolted from the bar.

Within an hour the boys at the other table began to disperse. Alex followed Bailey outside and shouted, "Hey, you with the red hair." Bailey turned around, flexed his biceps and snickered. He assured his friends, "Go on ahead. I'll catch up with you guys later." Bailey and Alex walked around the corner into the shadows. Bailey put both hands on his hips and sneered, "You're hangin' with that hot pussy, Betsy Howell. You cruisin' for a lickin'?"

Alex feigned an attack on the right and as Bailey went to counter, Alex darted around Bailey's left side and behind him, grabbed his ankle and lifted it sharply. Bailey fell face-first to the pavement. Alex turned him over and kicked him, twice, three times, four times, between his legs. He then grabbed Bailey's head, lifted it six inches off the ground and smashed it into the concrete. Bailey lapsed into unconsciousness. Alex unbuckled Bailey's belt and pulled his pants and underwear down to his knees in order to take more accurate aim. He kicked Bailey more than half a dozen times and stomped on him until Alex was out of breath. Alex stood up and started to walk away then turned around and planted his foot forcefully on Bailey's nose. He turned to leave again, but in two steps he found a length of narrow pipe. He picked it up and whacked it against Bailey's head. Then he turned Bailey over on his stomach, spread his cheeks and forced the pipe between them. He stood up, wiped his brow with his shirt sleeve and strode into the night.

Three days later, Betsy called, "Alex, do you want to take a walk and get some ice cream? Oh, and did you see the article in the *Daily Student*? The Deltas are saying it's Bailey Grogan."

Alex replied, "I saw it." He reread it to her:

"Tuesday night around 8:00 p.m. an Indiana University student was found in the alley just east of Tulagi. He was

savagely beaten and comatose. Local police suspect he was a victim of a gang attack. His identity was not disclosed by the university.

The student is recuperating in University Hospital, where his condition is listed as serious. He is non-responsive. Miss Halloway, dean of students, released the following statement: "It is the responsibility of this University to maintain a safe environment for students and faculty. Please provide any information you may have about this unfortunate incident to the Student Affairs Office in Robel Hall, Room 358, or call the Bloomington Police Department at (812) 327-3475."

Alex mused, "Too bad about that boy. His essential equipment is in a terrible state of disrepair. It won't be working for some time, if ever." Neither brought up the subject again.

Alex and Betsy were married after graduation in the backyard of the Howell estate. After a two-week honeymoon on the island of Mo'orea, they moved to Pittsburgh. Alex secured a job as a research intern at the University of Pittsburgh School of Medicine, where he began his studies in the fall of 1960. Betsy enjoyed the Morton family and Alex's high school chums and their spouses. Alex wanted to have children, but Betsy insisted they wait until they could settle down. After an internship and residency at Pittsburgh General Hospital, their next stop was Dallas, at MD Anderson for a fellowship in pediatric oncology. One night on the patio at Crab and Corn, referred to by the locals as "Crunchies" because of the hundreds of peanut shells strewn about the floor, as they shared a bottle of pinot noir, Betsy said to Alex, "We've been married eight years. I want to go home and raise a family."

CHAPTER EIGHT

The Fourth of July 1973 was a special occasion for the Howell family. Logan Howell and his wife, Emily, had celebrated their US citizenship less than ten years before. It did not take a trained linguist to recognize that the Howell family had emigrated from Quebec. Logan traced his family back to his great-great-grandfather, Logan Hywel, who had farmed the Irish countryside before emigrating to the New World. Logan's grandfather wore a mustache. He told Logan his own grandfather had grown one as well. Logan was not one to break the chain. Logan was of modest height, solid, and dense—thick. His sharp eye and intense gaze often unnerved his adversaries. He began his business with a single auto auction in Montreal. After he sold that auction to a public company owning multiple facilities, he was recruited to Indiana as its CEO. Within three years, he raised the capital to convert the company to private ownership and wound up with the majority share. Two years later he wheeled around and took the company public once more, under the name of "Howell on the Block."

The Howells lived on a twenty-acre estate replete with the amenities expected of a successful businessman. Logan had penetrated the social circle of business magnates from Cummins Engine, Eli Lilly, and Allison Transmission. Indianapolis Mayor Richard Lugar considered Logan a special business adviser.

By the time Alex and Betsy arrived at the Howells' that afternoon, the family celebration had begun. Logan cooked sirloin steaks on the outdoor grill while Betsy's siblings, Louis and Liam, and their families played Marco Polo in the pool.

Logan, who had grown up on ham hocks and potatoes, learned to appreciate a good cut of meat. He was a master at the grill. Emily had just concluded a five-mile run and was cooling off with her feet in the shallow end of the pool, talking with Alex's mother, Tina. Alex's father, Kevin, one of the most recent employees of Howell on the Block, relaxed in a lawn chair. The fathers-in-law bonded over their mutual interest in automobiles.

It was obvious to Alex that Betsy was Logan's favorite child. Like her father, she relished life when it was at its most exciting. Alex was delighted to join the Howell clan and appreciated the time that he and Logan spent together. Alex and Logan had developed a rapport—a mutual respect. Logan had felt that nobody could harness his daughter. She was full of life in such a delightful way. At the wedding, when Logan walked Betsy down the aisle and surrendered her to Alex, he whispered, "Alex, welcome to the family. Here's Betsy. You have no idea what you're getting into." Logan gave Alex a powder blue Corvette, among other wedding gifts from the Howell family.

After dinner, Alex, Kevin, Logan, and his sons, both of whom were in the family business, relaxed on the patio. Logan indulged in his only vice, a Cuban cigar. He inhaled ever so slightly and said, "Every Fourth of July I think how lucky I am to have such a wonderful family, and now, Betsy has come back home to us and I have a son-in-law. The community and the Almighty have been great to me."

From across the patio Betsy shouted, "And Mom!"

Logan laughed and shouted back, "And Mom! Of course, Mom." He turned to his younger son and asked, "Liam, how are the Racers doing?"

The Racers were the professional hockey team established in Indianapolis by the Howell family. They had purchased the team and moved it from Omaha, Nebraska, where it had been floundering. The team played in the ECHL, formerly known as the East Coast Hockey League, a midlevel minor league. Liam was queried on the subject at every family gathering. He replied to his father and the group, "The team looks good for the coming season. We signed a promising forward and a goalkeeper to replace Rifkin, that sieve with no teeth who was in the net most of last season. I think we can improve on our fourth-place finish, and maybe even compete for the Kelly Cup. Our attendance sucked last year. We have to fix that."

Logan twirled his mustache and blew another puff of smoke. He said, "Show Indy a winning team and you'll get all the support you dreamed of. That goes for any sport—hockey or soccer."

Louis held the title of vice president for advancement at the family auction house. The enhancement of the firm's capabilities was his responsibility. Last year, he deployed virtual lane technology at nearly half of the locations and added a platform allowing absentee dealers to buy and sell at every auction site. Louis sported a mustache. Liam did not.

Louis said, "Yes, the community has been good to us, but Dad, you have been good to the community as well. It is a mutual relationship."

Logan responded, "We can do more. Ever since we went public, I have been inundated with charitable requests. I started by accepting every one of them, from $100 to $5,000, but that's a poor strategy. We should make fewer contributions and focus on gifts that deliver more of an impact to this community."

Liam answered, "We are an important employer. We employ 670 people at our headquarters down the street and we donate at the highest level at United Way, where all three of us have served on the board. And what about our program providing financing for first-time auto owners? That's impactful."

"We do all of that and more, and I am perusing additional proposals, but none of them excite me very much."

In deference to Logan, Alex was nursing an iced tea with lemon instead of his normal summer weekend fare of a red wine spritzer. He said, "If you are looking for a gift that is meaningful, that can make an impact and help our community, Logan, I may have an idea for you."

Emily appeared and called all the guys together at the picnic table. "Dessert is served."

******

Alex was in Colson's office at 7:30 on Monday morning. "Functional" was the highest compliment one could pay to Colson's workspace, and that was barely deserved. Two area rugs covered spots where the wood floor could be seen through original carpet. Alex sat in a padded folding chair next to Colson's desk, which consisted of laminated plywood on a couple of "fancy" sawhorses. Alex began, "Marty, I'm glad we could get together on short notice. I have been burning with an idea. Have you developed a needs list for Rosenbaum that incorporates necessary repairs and improvements, and expenditures to maintain our competitiveness in pediatrics?"

Colson responded with feigned gravity, "Yes I have, your honor." He leaned back in his chair, opened his filing cabinet and extracted one of his light blue files. It read "Rosenbaum Need List." It was empty. He yelled to the chief financial officer, Rosanne Ross, to bring in the improvement and repair list. "Our CFO, Rosanne Ross, and I have prepared a list with cost estimates. We decided not to make the entire list public until we have at least a vague idea how to raise this kind of money." Alex and Rosanne were friends. They had collaborated on the recruitment phase of Alex's employment at Rosenbaum. Rosanne gave Alex the list. Alex glanced down to the bottom line. It read "$2,500,000." Almost a third of the number was allocated to roof repair. Items also included a data system upgrade, additional operating rooms, a nurse's lounge, and a children's play area. After Ross left, Alex closed the office door. He pulled his folding chair just a little closer to Colson and said, "Marty, I think I know where I can raise this money for us."

Colson responded, "If you can, I'll check with the Rosenbaum family about renaming the hospital."

Alex said, "No need for that, Marty, but there is a string attached. This must be kept in confidence. Just between the two of us, I think I can talk my father-in-law into a $3 million gift to Rosenbaum, but you have to promise me that you'll spend at least $500,000 to equip my lab on the sixth floor for state-of-the-art research on aging, including our progeria project."

Colson said, "What about my board of directors? What about the officers at the hospital? What about the physicians on staff? How can I possibly pull this off?"

Alex was prepared for those inquiries. He said, "Simply title a construction line 'laboratory upgrades.' We will need separate lab space with restricted access. We can call it the radioactive room. No one will dare go in there. You and I can control who will have access to that lab." Alex reached into his pocket and handed Marty a slip of paper. "Here's my list. With this equipment I don't need to run back to MD Anderson and beg for sophisticated microscope time. We can honor my father-in-law by renaming PP the 'Howell Conference Room' and add a nice portrait of Logan."

Colson was having trouble reining in his excitement. He said, "We can make room for that portrait by getting rid of some of those docs who passed away more than fifty years ago. I'll ask our attorney, David Wexler, to draw up the gift agreement and make sure we adhere to all the laws, rules, and regulations."

Alex stood, "Then we have a deal?"

Colson reached for Alex's hand and said, "Indeed we do."

CHAPTER NINE

"May we begin, Marty?"

Colson referred to his notes. "I think we are assembled for the most part." He slid his attendance chart across the table to David Wexler, recently named chairman of the Rosenbaum Advisory Board. "A few members could not make it today, and," Colson lowered his voice, "of course, Megan Wise is always late."

Colson leaned over to his chief financial officer, Rosanne Ross, and whispered, "Rosie, please do me a big favor. Go over to the Jester and ask him to put out his cigarette." Moments later the rustling of the Jester's candy wrapper could be heard before it fell to the floor.

The board consisted of 35 professionals and businessmen and -women between forty and seventy years of age—all hand-picked by Colson. A number of guests were present, including state officeholders. The board met in the largest meeting room at Rosenbaum—capacity sixty. It was an interior room and the hospital took advantage by adorning each wall with history. Framed newspaper articles, photographs of past board members and officers, photographs of all the physicians with hospital privileges, and plaques more numerous to count chronicled Rosenbaum's historic status. The room came to be called "the Pictures and Plaques Room," then just "Pictures and Plaques," then "the PP Room," and finally "PP." Colson had joked to Doc on the golf course one day that he was unable to grant privileges to another physician because there was no room for more photographs on the walls of PP.

In the center of the east wall was a portrait of the hospital's benefactor, Ike Rosenbaum. Isaiah (Ike) Rosenbaum was the first member of the Jewish faith to be offered staff privileges at Children's Hospital. He was respected and adored by his patients and their families. He was offered membership at the Columbine Club, the only Jew to receive an invitation. He rejected that offer without malice. He and his wife, Alice, had three children: two doctors and one lawyer. Alice survived Ike by ten years. When she died, she left her estate to the hospital. It was $3 million—all she had. In her will she declared her gift was made in accordance with her husband's wishes. The hospital was renamed Rosenbaum Children's Hospital. In respect for Rosenbaum's modesty, the legend under his picture read, "Isaiah (Ike) Rosenbaum, Physician."

"OK David, it's 4:05. Let's get started."

Wexler stood up and said, "Welcome to the October meeting of the Rosenbaum Advisory Board. We'll start by recognizing three new members. Please stand when I mention your name: John Roder, Betty Heisman, and Rob Salatich." All three stood to receive polite applause.

"Now I'll ask for a financial report," Wexler said.

"Just a minute." State Senator Micah Davis rose and pointed to Wexler. "Don't we want to start our meeting with an opening prayer?" Micah, in his late thirties, had just been re-elected to his second term in the legislature by energizing a voting bloc of conservative, homophobic voters. He had made national news with his comment that his own gay brother would probably burn in hell. He wore a full beard and sported a bow tie that bounced on his Adam's apple as he spoke.

"Micah, I know this board has begun its meeting with prayer from time to time, but that is the chairman's prerogative. It's a bad practice that usually emphasizes our differences and does little to encourage the collaboration we need at these meetings. As your new board chairman, I have dispensed with this tradition. In its place, I will allow a moment of silence."

Micah Davis was silent, but Wexler read the disdain on his face.

After a minute Wexler began again, "Now the financial report. Mrs. Ross, please."

Ross was in her twentieth year with Rosenbaum, ten as the CFO. More than CFO, she was an integral member of the Colson management team and an advocate for the doctors on staff. Everyone called her Rosie.

She stood, slightly stooped with papers in hand. She exchanged greetings while she distributed financial information to each table. Ross brushed away a few gray strands from her forehead and peered over her reading glasses. "I am pleased to report donations in September continued the robust trend we experienced throughout the summer. As you can see, our results of operations are strong. The "Send Jimmy to Disneyland" fund stands at $748.50, and the side yard tree planting initiative has raised $1,500. You can dedicate a tree in honor of anyone you wish for a contribution of $500. There are ten spots left. The Rawls Minority Scholarship Fund is nearly depleted. Please help us with that. Our speaker next month will be Dr. Bella Bradford-Baker, the first recipient of a full scholarship from the Rawls Fund.

Thanks to the Howell grant, our modernization initiative is in full swing, including window replacement and new furniture in our patient lounges. Perhaps that explains the continued uptick in donations. What you do not see in this material is the glaring need for roof repair. Our latest estimate has been reduced to $775,000. We'll get most of this from the Howell grant, but we are seeking to identify a donor for the rest. I ask you, who wants to put his name on a roof? It's only one step up from naming the men's urinal."

Wexler brought a stop to the levity with a curt, "Thank you for your report. We will hold a formal dedication and renaming ceremony for this room as soon as the portrait of Logan Howell has been completed." Wexler was a corporate and tax attorney, fifteen years into a successful career. He was comfortable in the corporate boardroom and on the golf course, where he spent Wednesday, Saturday and Sunday afternoons. He had played number four on the golf team at Purdue University. That enthusiasm and his propensity to leverage his tall athletic frame and shaggy brown hair for a frenetic social life made admission to law school a crapshoot, according to his father. He was accepted by Indiana University School of Law, which operated with this policy, "We take you, but beware: If you don't do well, we will flunk you out." Wexler understood. He excelled, but his handicap burgeoned to an eight.

Colson recruited Wexler for his business acumen, his Rolodex, and his arm-twisting skills. He was Colson's personal attorney and had been for more than a decade. The word in the doctor's lounge was that Wexler's clients minimized taxes. It was said he knew all the tricks.

Wexler went to the next item on his agenda.

"Do we have an announcement on our Christmas dinner?"

Colson stood up. "We do, Mr. Chair. I have undertaken the responsibility this year because I wanted to make a few changes. First, there will be no "Christmas Dinner." From now on we'll call it "Holiday Dinner," and second, we will not hold our celebration at Madison Woods Country Club this year or any year until that institution opens its doors to members without regard to race or religion. We'll let you know in November where we will hold our party." Micah Davis rose to object, looked around and silently sat back down in his chair.

Wexler had discussed this endeavor with Colson and was not surprised. His smile conveyed approval. Wexler continued, "Marty, now that you have the floor, please introduce our guest speaker."

Megan Wise slipped in just as Colson began.

"It is my honor to introduce Dr. Alex Morton. Dr. Morton majored in zoology at Indiana University. He graduated from medical school at the University of Pittsburgh in 1964 and joined us four years ago after completing a fellowship at MD Anderson in Dallas. He is a pediatric oncologist with a research emphasis in molecular and cellular biology. He heads our Institute on Aging and runs our fellowship program. He and his wife, Betsy Howell Morton, are avid skiers. In 1973, Betsy received the Presidential Citizens Medal for her work in raising awareness of sexual assault on college campuses. The couple resides in Carmel. Today Dr. Morton has promised to provide us with a primer on biology and a glimpse into some of the projects we are working on here at Rosenbaum. Dr. Morton."

Alex stood and acknowledged the applause. He fired up his slide show.

"Thank you, Dr. Colson. It is a pleasure for me to live and work and hopefully raise a family in Indiana. I have often been asked 'Why Indiana? Was it our special hospital? The money? Dr. Colson's charm?' I'll tell you a secret. I was recruited to head pediatrics at Duke University with a shot to serve someday as dean of its medical school. I love Duke. Did I mention they threw in two season tickets for the Duke Blue Devils basketball games? Rosenbaum made a nice offer too—chairmanship of a new Center of Excellence in pediatric oncology. When I discussed these opportunities with my wife Betsy, she responded immediately, 'That's great, but you need to know one thing. If you are going to Duke, you are going alone.' Ladies and gentlemen, here we are in Indiana!

"Our Center of Excellence in pediatric oncology has morphed into the Institute on Aging. I was drawn into the field of geronomics, the study of aging's basic biology, when I was given the opportunity to treat"—Alex raised a finger, "maybe, just maybe cure—a thirty-month-old boy who was diagnosed with progeria, a despicable malady that ages children at ten times the normal rate. These kids almost always die in their teens. When we undertook this responsibility, nothing much was known about progeria and, in fact, very little was known about the normal aging process. The history of aging research has had more than its share of workers of questionable integrity and limited talent. It was considered a researcher dead end. I felt that was a false conclusion. The area presented enormous questions that had not been approached precisely and aggressively.

I realize many of you already know the information I'm about to present, but this may be new to some. Just to make sure we all start on the same page, let's begin this talk at a basic level." Alex showed the first slide. He said, "What do you see here?"

The screen was white.

"No, it's not a white house in a snowstorm. It's an atom, the smallest unit of matter. Every single living thing is made up of atoms. You can't see it because it cannot be seen by the naked eye." Alex flipped to the next slide. It was the same white background with many dots in the middle of the screen.

"This is what a molecule would look like if you possessed microscopic vision. A molecule is a combination of atoms."

The next slide depicted a black sphere on the white background. "This is a cell, the building block of life. It is estimated that there are 100 trillion atoms in a single cell and 100 trillion cells in our bodies.

Alex followed that slide with a photograph of Raquel Welch's famous cheesecake pose. "Can anyone identify this slide?" The women groaned. Alex thought, "I am totally out of line here. Betsy was right. That's it for Raquel." Alex continued with his lecture. "Now picture Raquel as just a mass of 100 trillion cells. How about this? Alex's next slide was Martin Colson. Our friend Dr. Colson also has 100 trillion cells, give or take one or two.

Our research at Rosenbaum begins at the cellular level, so let's take another look at that cell." The black sphere with the white background popped up again, with labels.

Cell

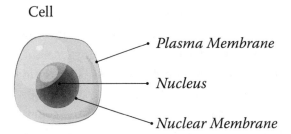

Plasma Membrane

Nucleus

Nuclear Membrane

The plasma membrane allows things to move in and out of the cell. Let's break through that plasma membrane and look inside the cell at the nucleus:

Nucleus

Nuclear Membrane

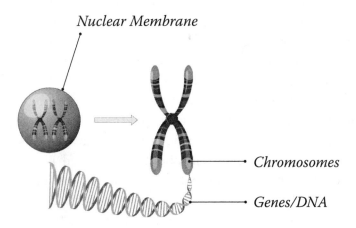

Chromosomes

Genes/DNA

For every cell except for red blood cells, there are 46 chromosomes inside the nucleus: twenty-three from dad and twenty-three from mom."

Alex went on, "Chromosomes are structures within the nucleus that contain a person's genes; and genes, in turn, are segments of deoxyribonucleic acid. Don't worry if you cannot pronounce that. Doctors have trouble with it too. That's why we all refer to it as DNA. Our traits are determined by our genes, and the genes are coded by our DNA. It's the genes we are primarily interested in at the Institute on Aging. Genes are the chemical blueprints within cells. Each gene consists of a coded chemical message that directs the cell to produce a particular protein necessary either for body structure or for a metabolic process. They guide the development of an animal from a fertilized egg to adulthood. Genes turn off and on at different times to carry out the genetic program. They may guide the body through aging as well. There are more than 50,000 genes that control human life and health. If we could identify the location of a defective gene, we might be able to tailor its repair or replace it altogether.

The study of aging here at Rosenbaum presents opportunities for staggering discoveries. We are dealing with questions of why we age, how we age, and how we prevent aging. Think about it this way. Aging is the process of increasing vulnerability to many diseases that lead to death. Therefore, slowing down the aging process will lead to a longer life. Simple studies affecting aging have dealt with severe lifestyle changes, including under-nourishment and body temperature reduction. It is clear that calorie restriction in some species will lead to a life span up to 50 percent longer. It has been long suspected that humans can achieve that outcome. It has also been noted that these species suffer a weakened immune system and a lower sex drive in this scenario. Humans would probably suffer those outcomes as well." Alex displayed his next slide, a skeleton in a tuxedo blowing out candles on a birthday cake with a caption "Happy 150th Birthday."

"Now may be a good time to invest in candles," Alex added with a chuckle. He was rolling, and continued with increasing energy. "We also have credible evidence that if we lower our body temperature, we can add multiple years to our lives. It works with roundworms and fish in cold water, and there is anecdotal evidence of a well-aged society of yogis in India who have achieved this result."

The next slide depicted a shivering male standing outside an igloo in Bermuda shorts and shirt sleeves.

"Anyone up for a winter home north of the Arctic Circle? These concepts are interesting experiments of little value, as far as they go. We continue to engage in these studies with our students as a means to teach scientific methods and rigorous discipline in the experimental process. Speaking of students, there is a theory that blood transfusion from young donors will extend our life spans. This is one of many ideas we may investigate.

Our focus is retarding or curing progeria and perchance extending the human life span, perhaps reversing the aging process altogether. The study of telomeres has been fascinating in this regard."

The slide of the nucleus flashed up on the screen again, with an added label for telomeres. Alex explained:

Nucleus

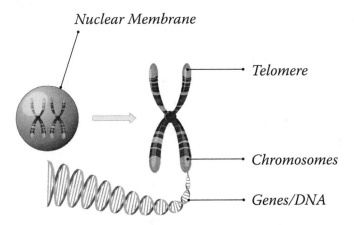

"Telomeres are pieces of DNA that cap the chromosomes. These caps keep our chromosomes from unraveling, much like the plastic tips at the end of our shoelaces. Cells go through a process of dividing called mitosis. Every time a cell divides, its telomeres get shorter, like a fuse burning down to its end. Once a cell runs out of telomeres, as it does with age and in some diseases, it can't reproduce anymore and dies. What if we could bathe our cells in a solution that would prevent our telomeres from getting shorter? Would our cells continue to reproduce? Would we live forever? Could we wind back the biological clock?

"Some people view the human body as a well-oiled machine. I look at it as a battleground in a skirmish that today it is destined to lose. Does that have to be the case? Perhaps old age is an illness that we can tame, like measles and polio. Today, no magic potions or genetic engineering exist. No serious scientist believes in immortality. But maybe, just maybe, death is a problem we can delay. Progress is being made. A baby born in the U.S. today can realistically look forward to living to 100. Maybe the first human to live 150 years has already been born." Alex closed out the slide set and readied to make his closing statement.

Micah Davis popped up before Alex had a chance to summarize. Micah pointed a finger at Alex and declaimed, "Read your Bible, Dr. Morton. God created this earth and every living creature, including you and me. He gave man a life span of three score and ten and woman to share that life in a sacred union of holy marriage. For those of us who make it to heaven, God has granted eternal bliss. There is no reason for the righteous among us to delay this ecstasy. Your investigations are an assault on human nature, contrary to God's intention, are sacrilegious and will lead to ruin."

The Jester blew his nose loudly.

Turning to the head table, Davis said, "Dr. Colson, as CEO of this hospital you need to put a stop to this waste of our resources and utter madness without delay. Mr. Wexler, I hereby formally request a full report on this matter at your next meeting." Micah Davis folded his arms across his chest, looked around the room for approval, found none and sat down.

Wexler ran his hand through his shaggy brown hair and sighed. "I'll make a note, Micah."

Alex replied, "Mr. Davis, I respect your religious beliefs and your right to express them. I also believe in a supreme being, but I have a different point of view. I believe God has bestowed upon us certain gifts—gifts of intelligence and curiosity, among many others. He has enabled us and expects us to seek answers to our lives on this earth, including our deaths—to answer the grand question, "What exactly is the limit of the human life span?" The God I worship would be disappointed if I did not use these gifts to help our society and future generations enjoy longer and healthier lives. The gifts from God of radical long life are at our feet all wrapped up in a large box. We just have to figure out how to take the ribbon off.

Now, let me make a final plea to all of you. As we raise the profile of our Institute on Aging, we need to continue to focus on raising money to support our scientific studies, including providing fellowships for outstanding graduate candidates. We will need to purchase sophisticated equipment to aid us in this research, equipment that no one had even conceived of as little as three years ago. I suspect this will be an ongoing challenge. We are committed to create and maintain a Center of Excellence at the Institute on Aging at Rosenbaum and under the guidance and leadership of Dr. Colson, we will do just that. Thank you for your assistance so far and for honoring me with this invitation to speak with you today." Alex was treated to standing applause.

CHAPTER TEN

Janie curled up on Doc's lap one November evening while they were enjoying a fire in the family room.

"Hon, why don't we invite a few people over to share Thanksgiving dinner this year?"

"Janie, let's not. Last year was wonderful with just the three of us—you, Brenda, and me."

"Well, it's too late, dear. Brenda asked if she could spend Thanksgiving at a friend's house, and I've already invited the Thompsons. You know Margo, and she's married to that bright young lawyer, George Taylor. You and Margo can talk about chicken pox, and I'll talk to George about the statute of limitations."

"What do you know about the statute of limitations?"

"Nothing. While we're at it, why don't we include Ralph Jessup? He's all by himself, and Thanksgiving is not a time to be all by yourself."

"Have you already invited him?"

"Yep."

The guests arrived about the same time. Margo handed Janie a bouquet of fall flowers. Janie said, "Come with me into the kitchen while I find a vase for these splendid flowers. Thank you. The guys can go into the family room. Where is George?"

"We're separated."

"I'm so sorry."

"We have religious differences."

"Religious differences? I thought you were both Baptists."

"Yes, but he thought he was God and I didn't. It's my fault. He was a clumsy lab partner. I should have known."

A bell sounded. Janie opened the oven door. Margo said, "That turkey smells just like home. Momma's favorite place in the house was the kitchen. She served up our turkey with cracklins and red beans."

"Next year come over early and we'll try some of your mother's recipes."

Janie pointed at the kitchen counter. "Margo, grab two of those oven mittens and help me, please."

The women wrestled the turkey onto the cutting block. Janie called, "Milt, come into the kitchen. The turkey is ready to be carved." Janie offered him a large fork and cutting knife.

Doc dropped the knife before it even hit the turkey. Janie handed him a second knife and Doc began the process—legs and wings first. When he dropped a wing on the floor, Margo stepped forward, "Doc, thank God you decided not to become a surgeon. Hand over your weapons." Margo finished the carving project without further incident.

After dinner and pumpkin pie, everyone cleared the dishes and then relaxed in the family room. Janie announced, "When I was growing up, in my house, we had a ritual." She reached into a sack and presented her two guests with wild turkey feathers. Doc got one too. "We had to earn our turkey feathers by recalling a memorable Thanksgiving moment." Janie brushed her feather across Doc's nose with a gentle touch. "I remember the time all the kids, including cousins from out of town, argued over who could break the wishbone. When I was given a chance, I grasped that bone and made a fervent wish, but I ended up with the short end. Thank God all my wishes came true when I married Doc. How about you, Ralph? Would you like to earn your turkey feather?"

"I don't know, Janie. My Thanksgiving memories aren't so happy."

"I didn't say 'happy.' I said *memorable*."

"This will be difficult for me. But OK, I am among friends and I have shared some of this already with Doc.

"I remember the winter of 1950, or it seemed like winter. I had graduated that past June from Ohio State in a pre-med curriculum. I loved the sciences and, I know it's unusual, but organic chemistry was a favorite. I grew up in Bexley, a suburb of Columbus, Ohio. I was kind of shy, and I didn't venture too far from home.

"Because of my grades and scores I was accepted to the Indiana University School of Medicine, but upon the recommendation of my chemistry professor, Marek Fludzinski, I chose a year of research and study in Boston. Obtaining a deferment from IU was no problem, but my draft board had other ideas. There was that "police action" in Korea and I guess they needed live bodies. The board was notified I was no longer in school, and the next thing I knew, I was in boot camp. I still have never been to Boston.

"The Army gave me fatigues, a burr haircut and a free ride to Seoul. I hoped it would be a round trip. I cursed my bad judgment and that of my draft board. I thought, 'Could I have the worst draft board in America?' Then I met a fellow recruit with one eye. He washed out of boot camp. I did not.

"Many was the day I wished I were in a science lab conducting experiments or dissecting bodies. As it turned out, bodies became my specialty. I asked to be assigned to hospital administration. When that didn't pan out, I requested attachment to a MASH unit as an orderly, or a doctor's assistant. In the great wisdom of the Army desk jockeys back home, I was designated a Graves Registration service officer assigned to mortuary affairs with the 148th G.R.

"After battles had been won—or lost—we were dispatched to place our fallen comrades in body bags and helicopter them back to base camp. Occasionally, we had to bury them where they lay and mark their graves for reburial later. My orders tasked me with retrieval, identification, transportation, and burial of deceased American and allied military personnel. It was gruesome. We were trained in first aid, but we were always too late. I often had to body-bag friends or parts of friends. Some bodies were completely destroyed, and I'd have to pick up pieces of skull and tissue. Then, there was always the chance that bodies were booby-trapped with trip wires to grenades. I shook with fright from the moment I disembarked from the helicopter to the time I was returned safely to our base camp at Wonju, about fifty miles from the front lines.

"The Wonju flag always flew at half-staff in honor of the bodies on site. Wonju was in the war zone, but amidst the frenetic activity of logistical deployments of men and materiel, it was sometimes downright tranquil. There was squalor and rust and mud. The odor of fuel competed with the smell of human excrement wafting from a sanitary sewer system inadequate to keep up with the upsurge in personnel. Yet one could also find beauty. Flowers persisted in vibrant colors. I would gaze at the bright orange twilight lilies, and they would afford me moments of peace. Most nights I could not sleep.

"We were labeled post-combat soldiers, not combat soldiers, but we were assigned revolvers. Standard issue was the .45 Colt model 1911A1 sidearm. The weapons were provided to Mortuary Affairs personnel with a strong recommendation that they never leave our holsters. I was comforted to pack the pistol during our body forays. You see, there was really no such thing as post combat when you were at the front in Korea.

"Before Thanksgiving time, and I don't recall the exact date, military bulletins declared that we would be visited by the USO. The hot poop was it would be in the person of Bob Hope and his entourage. It would be Hope's first trip to Korea, and we were excited to enjoy Thanksgiving turkey with all the trimmings and entertainment by Bob Hope and a bunch of semi-naked dancing girls." The Jester tilted his head toward Margo and Janie. "Remember, I was in my early 20s. We were all to be flown in to Won San, an airfield that had just been established. At the last minute our battalion executive officer, a ninety-day wonder, removed some of us from the troop list and ordered us to stand by for duty later that night. You can imagine how disappointed we were. One of my fellow battlefield GRs told the officer to 'blow it out his barracks bag.' Luckily, the lieutenant laughed it off. Instead of turkey I had C-rations. I remember trading a can of ham and lima beans for spaghetti.

"I lay on my cot that night in Wonju listening to the Seoul City Sue radio announcer and feeling rotten about my situation. At 2:00 a.m. we departed by Sioux helicopter under a full moon. In many ways that was scarier than darkness, as we could be seen by the enemy if any of them were still lurking. The protocol: collect and beat feet out of there. Usually, by the time I reboarded the Sioux, I was soaked with sweat."

The Jester paused to wipe his face with a napkin. He took a breath and began again. "That night had seen a harsh, devastating battle. We picked our way among the bodies, found our own and began gathering them up. I was upset. I had missed the turkey and I had missed Bob Hope. I had identified a comrade-in-arms and had to pick up his pieces and load them into a body bag. When you are in a war, the guys you are with are like a fraternity. You get close during a war. I cursed the enemy that was responsible for the loss of my friend. I hated the Gooks. Gook was a dehumanizing term that was brainwashed into us during indoctrination to desensitize us to killing our fellow man. I would never use that term today, nor anything like it. The officers had me pegged when I got there as a Midwestern boy who might be a dangerous pacifist."

The Jester tapped his fingers on the side table in rapid cadence. He leaned back in his chair and closed his eyes. "Does anyone have a cigarette?"

Janie said, "Ralph, you've earned your feather, let's stop here and I'll serve the eggnog."

"Janie, I need to finish the story. My buddies were loading up the last body bag when I heard rustling about twenty yards from me at the edge of the clearing. We trained to be hypersensitive to signs of enemy activity both in daylight and at night. I heard it again. It seemed to come from high up in a tree between me and the moon. I unholstered my revolver and advanced a number of paces. When I heard the rustle above me, I aimed into the moon and fired three shots. A body landed at my feet. It wasn't a Gook. It was a little Korean girl in a dark blue dress." The Jester began to cry. He sobbed. He closed his eyes and reached in his right front pocket for a piece of candy and put it in his mouth. He then extracted the wrapper.

Margo put her arm around the Jester's shoulders and hugged him. She said softly, "You are a compassionate man. We love you."

The Jester fought to recover his composure. He said, "I woke up in the Seoul military hospital—the psych ward. They diagnosed 'operational exhaustion' and cut orders to ship me back to the States on a wacko discharge, but I prevailed and they transferred me to hospital administration. That was what I had requested in the first place.

"I have replayed that incident in my mind a hundred times, the rustling in the trees and the thud of that little girl at my feet. I have flashbacks and nightmares. I remember all the things that happened that night and I always will—Thanksgiving, the mission, the battlefield in the moonlight, the little girl, and the spaghetti."

The Jester sat up and opened his eyes. He wiped his brow with his handkerchief. "I started med school in January after my hitch was up. I was too busy to make new friends, or maybe I just didn't care. I felt somehow detached—emotionally numb. After that horrible episode I decided to become a pediatrician. Rosenbaum Children's Hospital was just right for me. To live in freedom is a costly privilege. My psychiatrist says I paid my share. I don't think the bill will ever be repaid."

Janie brought a tray of eggnogs and a bottle of brandy from the kitchen. She presented the sack of turkey feathers to the Jester and said, "You are my new true friend and this will be my most memorable Thanksgiving."

CHAPTER ELEVEN

"Dr. Adams?"

Mary tapped lightly on the examining room door. When he opened it, she whispered, "I squeezed in one more patient this afternoon. After you are through with Eli, I need some direction."

Mary caught him in the hall between patients.

"Milt, Deborah Higgins needs you to sign the standard release form for new students in Washington Township schools. Little Jimmy is starting school and she just decided to enroll him at Crooked Creek Elementary. As you know, Dr. Thompson is Jimmy's primary pediatrician. She is out of town and the form is required before the first day of school, which is Tuesday. Since Dr. Morton has confined his care to the progeria and related difficulties, his office suggested Mrs. Higgins call us. I informed her of our policy of not signing those forms without a current physical exam."

Doc beamed. "Good thinking, Mary. I'd be honored to sign the form. When is he coming in?"

"Two-thirty. What shall I do with him?"

"Put him in our waiting room just like any other kid. If he is going to be mainstreamed, he is going to have to get used to gawking and pointing. I know some children can be cruel, but Jimmy will have to endure it. After one week in school his oddness will melt away."

Doc took care to be ready to see the young boy as soon as he arrived. Jimmy walked down the hall and into the waiting room holding his mother's hand. His gait was stiff-kneed, as though he had just dismounted a horse. He wore soft-soled slippers, easing the discomfort of his bent, sensitive toes. His posture was stooped, as though he would fall forward without his mother's support. He elicited stares as he labored through the waiting room, where he was met by Mary, who gathered preliminary data. She ushered him into an examining room, where Doc welcomed him with both arms outstretched. Jimmy presented exactly like Doc expected, but Doc was shocked by Mrs. Higgins. She had turned completely gray.

"Mrs. Higgins, it's so nice to see you. You and your husband must be so proud that your son is starting school. I remember when Crooked Creek was a little red schoolhouse and now it's a modern, fully equipped facility."

Deborah Higgins gave her son's hand a squeeze. "I am proud. Mr. Higgins is too, but he chose to move to California."

Doc turned his attention to his patient. "Jimmy, I haven't seen you for years. We met when you were around two when your mother brought you to the hospital. I remember you were upset with me when I tried to examine you. Come on in and take off your hat. We'll get started."

Deborah Higgins nodded. "I remember that day, Dr. Adams." She wiped away a tear.

Jimmy spoke in a shrill voice. "I don't remember, Doc, but I'm not upset with you now. Just no shots. Oh, I heard you hand out lollipops." He gave his Fighting Irish cap to his mother.

"OK Jimmy, no shots."

Jimmy was only six, but progeria was already exacting a heavy toll. Jimmy presented as a bald, wrinkled old man. Blueish veins were prominent on his naked scalp. Jimmy looked exactly like the photograph in Doc's father's medical textbook. He had a beaked nose and little elephant ears. His eyes were outsized, but bore the deep, unmistakable sign of above-average intelligence.

The medical exam included close observation of bones and joints—probable progeria targets. It was otherwise routine. Mary handed Doc a note. Doc read the note and turned to Mrs.

Higgins. "Jimmy weighed in today at 38 pounds. That's consistent with prior exams. He is holding steady. He should be on a battery of vitamins and other supplements."

Mrs. Higgins handed Doc a list. She replied, "I thought you would ask. He also goes into Rosenbaum once a month for intravenous nutritional enrichment therapy that includes growth-hormones. We are following the advice of the Rosenbaum nutritionists and providing frequent small meals to increase Jimmy's maximum calorie intake."

Doc continued, "Mrs. Higgins, my assistant talked to Dr. Thompson's office. Dr. Thompson could not be reached, but her assistant thought Jimmy's inoculations were up to date. Schools today, like always, are concerned with communicable diseases, including mumps, measles, and chicken pox. Please double-check with Dr. Thompson when she is back in the office. Those childhood ailments and even the common cold can be especially dangerous for Jimmy. I noticed Jimmy has an early-stage cataract in his left eye. Mary will give you the business card of Dr. Spitz. Jimmy ought to have a thorough eye exam at this point.

"There won't be enough room for all those teeth that are erupting. I suggest you consult with Dr. Lambert Smith to sort that out. There may be a need for selective extraction. Dr. Smith is painless. He's a special guy who provides more pro bono work than any dentist in town. Mary has his contact information as well. Book the appointment through his assistant, Patty Kay. Everybody calls her Punky. Jimmy's joints are stiff but that is to be expected, given his condition. Did Dr. Thompson prescribe a daily aspirin for pain relief and as a pre-emptive strike at his heart disease?"

Mrs. Higgins put her arm around her son's shoulder and said, "Do you know that guy on TV, Jack LaLanne? Jimmy watches him and tries to keep up. Every morning Jimmy and I stretch his limbs and work on flexibility. It seems to help his arthritis a little and yes, an aspirin is part of Jimmy's daily regimen."

With a wink to Mrs. Higgins, Doc said, "Jimmy, no shots today. Do you or your mother have any questions?"

Jimmy sat up on the examining table and focused knowing eyes on Doc. He said, "I asked my doctors to make my condition go away. Dr. Thompson said I need to make the best of the situation and she would help me. Dr. Morton said, 'Don't give up hope. I am working on it.'

"I want to be like the other kids. Please, can you help me?"

"Jimmy, I don't know how to make this go away. I sure wish I could, but if there is something to be done, your two doctors will find it. Tell me about your activities."

Mary tapped on the door and stuck her head in. "Dr. Adams, you have patients waiting."

"A few more minutes, Mary."

Jimmy replied, "I love music, but I don't sing so well. I like the Eagles. Mom likes them too. She says they were a hit while I was still in diapers. I like sports. I went to the Indianapolis 500 Mile Race last year, well, maybe 300 miles of it. At home, I play with my Legos. I made the London Bridge. I quit violin lessons. The violin sounds too much like I talk. I like to read."

Mrs. Higgins held Jimmy's hand and said, "Dr. Adams, Jimmy is already reading at first-grade level. He is excited for school."

"Mom reads to me almost every night. My favorite story is Pinocchio. It's about a wooden puppet who gets in all kinds of trouble. He gets swallowed by a whale and he has a conscience named Jiminy Cricket, kinda like my name, and he became a real boy.

"I want to become a real boy."

CHAPTER TWELVE

Doc and Janie were on their way to play bridge at the home of Alex and Betsy—and what a home. It was in a gated Carmel neighborhood. The home was rumored to have been a gift from Betsy's father, Logan, who provided like gifts for all three of his children, along with ample trust funds.

As they drove, Janie rattled off instructions for proper behavior. The closer they got to their destination, the more intense the directives became. "Milt, please don't say anything about their house. I've been there. It's over the top. Just be cool. And Milt dear, try to keep hospital gossip and medical mumbo jumbo to a minimum. There should be plenty of other topics to amuse you. The Yossos will be there. He'll want to talk about himself, his last 1,000 deliveries or his hole-in-one. Golf is boring. Try to keep him off that track."

Janie continued as they proceeded up the driveway. It was a quarter-mile long, but it seemed longer to Milt. By the time they reached the front porch, Janie was not finished. She just ran out of breath. Betsy answered the door.

Two steps into the foyer, Doc looked up at the chandelier hanging from the high ceiling and exclaimed a little too loudly, "Wow, Betsy, what a house."

Janie glared at Doc while she handed Betsy a bottle of New Zealand chardonnay.

The other guests were already seated. Doc was always late to Friday night engagements. He couldn't seem to treat those last few children and close up shop before six o'clock. He and Mary were usually locking up around seven.

Betsy planned two bridge tables to include the Yossos and Marty and Teddi Colson.

Bridge at the social level was not difficult for either Doc or Alex, particularly the play of the hand. Both men were intuitive and good decision-makers. Bidding was another matter. Doc didn't devote the effort to memorizing rules and conventions. His undisciplined communication resulted in unmakeable contracts for Janie to suffer through. Usually, by the end of the night her patience with Doc was drained. Bastardizing a term from tennis, Janie referred to their bridge outings as "mixed troubles."

At the other table the Yossos and the Colsons played a more sophisticated game. Melanie Yosso played duplicate bridge and Teddi and Marty Colson played in a regular foursome. Doc responded to Janie's pleas to play more often, like the Colsons, with the comment, "Marty is in administration. He's got the time."

Ward Yosso was an obstetrician with a "society" practice who counted many of his patients in Alex's neighborhood. His colleagues referred to him as "Goldfinger." Some of his patients referred to him as "Dreamy Blue Eyes." He was bald. Not balding with thin hair and a comb-over, but completely bald with a shaved head, and as many patients said, the more handsome for it. He had not yet surrendered that quick step of youth, perhaps due to the weekly singles tennis game with coach Tyler of the Carmel High School team. In the evening he sported a cane as a fashion statement. It was silver tipped with a hooded cobra head at the top. The cane lent credence to the handicap parking permit Yosso had finagled. He was nearing the end of his OB years. He estimated that he had delivered more than 5,000 babies and circumcised nearly a quarter of them. His patients loved him. Some too much. At fifty-three years of age, he had no enthusiasm for midnight hospital runs. He continued his GYN work, specializing in infertility, particularly artificial insemination.

Janie had just gone down three in a doubled contract after Doc had leapt to seven hearts. The partnership was missing two aces. Betsy sensed the tension and stood up. She stepped to the next table and said, "Melanie, finish that hand. We're going to take a break."

Alex left the room and returned with a translucent container about one-inch square. The top appeared to be minutely perforated. He unsnapped the lid and tilted the contents onto the middle of Betsy's bridge table.

Betsy covered her mouth and exclaimed, "You brought this filthy mess into my house?"

Alex laughed. "Filthy mess? I want to introduce you to my friend Wormer von Braun and his family." Everyone gathered round what appeared to be the droppings of a small puppy.

Yosso asked, "Do you mean Wernher von Braun? He was a Nazi missile-builder. My great-uncle lost his life in a bombing raid trying to put this monster's V-2 rocket factory out of business. Instead of prosecuting him for war crimes, the good old USA brought him and his team of Nazis to our shores to jump-start our program of weapons and space travel. He was never punished for his evil deeds."

"No, Yos, I mean *Wormer* von Braun, a lowly worm advancing ideas in a different space."

Doc broke in, "That small pile of brown you refer to as Wormer and family are nematodes, aren't they? Nematodes, or as we call them, 'roundworms,' have been shown repeatedly to hold lessons for humans, despite the evolutionary distance between the two species. These guys mature and reproduce quickly. They only live about three weeks, so experimental conclusions can be reached with greater speed." Friends had ceased to be amazed at the depth and breadth of Doc's knowledge of all things medical.

Melanie Yosso wondered out loud, "Why is all your research on aging done with animals that aren't very good at it? Why not concentrate on animals that are good at aging, like elephants, and then figure out how they do it?" She offered another thought. "Why is my cat, Tessa, who gets plenty of exercise and doesn't smoke or drink, condemned to die after about ten years, and you live on for many more decades?"

Doc replied, "It is difficult to perform scientific studies in most organisms due to their long lives. As for why some animals live longer than others, no one really knows for sure."

Alex continued, "Nematodes are hermaphrodites that produce egg and sperm. Wormer is capable of self-fertilization."

Melanie looked around and said, "Girls, let's join the nematodes. Penises will be irrelevant!"

Teddi Colson chimed in, "Were they ever relevant?"

Marty parried, "I heard they were sure relevant to you in college."

Teddi acted hurt. "That's an evil accusation. I was not easy!" She paused and sipped her wine. "But I wasn't impossible." She winked at Yosso. Teddi was a blond—a real blond. Yosso knew that. Her wardrobe reflected her pride in maintaining her college figure. Everyone knew that.

Marty met Teddi during his first year of residency at Methodist Hospital. Teddi saw Marty as a perfect capstone to her nursing "career." As they sipped coffee in the hospital cafeteria in the midst of his all-night rotation, Marty said, "Are there any more flashy-dashy blondes from Crawfordsville, Indiana?"

"No Marty, I'm the only one." Teddi started to add more when Marty's pager lit up.

"Gotta go. It's two a.m. and I'm already beat. I can't wait to go back to sleep."

"Where's that?"

"Room B20."

"I'll keep your bed warm for you."

They were married within a year.

Alex enjoyed Marty and Teddi's banter, but he wasn't finished with his science lesson. "Not so fast, ladies. Nematodes still prefer to mate with real males."

Betsy chimed in. "Wouldn't we all."

Teddi could match Betsy quip for quip. Friends say she was "active" in college at Ball State's School of Nursing. No further explanation was given—none was required.

Yosso followed the conversation with interest. Teddi was his patient. He thought, "definitely not a UFO." UFO—ugly, fat, and offensive—was a term Yosso often entered in his patients' charts. He thought, "Doc and Alex would be appalled at my rating system." Yosso looked forward to Teddi's regular appointments.

Alex whispered, "Yos, don't forget to send me that foreskin tissue you promised."

Yosso whispered back, "My last two families buried the foreskin in their backyard as part of a Jewish ritual. Those crazy Jews. Of course, I am one of them. I'll send you a package next week."

Alex added more details. "An experiment back in the '30s proved that a 30 percent calorie restriction could increase the life span of these creatures by up to 50 percent. I don't think anyone ever proved it could work in humans, because people found it impossible to maintain such a diet. They viewed the under-nourished routine as a subtraction from life, not an addition. Swapping food for time works. It's just unpleasant."

Betsy piped up, "Don't ask me to try such a crazy thing. By the way, I'm serving strawberry cheesecake for dessert tonight."

Doc asked, "Alex, are you thinking calorie restriction is a key to your progeria protocol?"

"No, Milt. Dietary restriction is not appropriate for progeria therapy. Little Jimmy weighs less than 40 pounds as it is. He needs continual enriched nourishment. Margo has him on a pile of vitamins, including monthly intravenous supplements. It may be possible one day to give Jimmy and all of us a pill to make the body think it is on a calorie restrictive diet and thus derive the same benefits. That could have far-reaching effects. There may already be a drug like that. Are you aware of the 'French paradox?' Why is it that the French eat a high-fat diet without affecting their longevity? Maybe it's a chemical in all that red wine they drink? Maybe in the grapes?

"Everyone is pretty sure there is a substance or treatment that can retard aging, but where is it? An anti-aging pill would be the ultimate blockbuster drug. No single drug like that has ever been contemplated. There is always the potential with new drug treatment that it may stop aging—by killing the patient. Right now, our work on aging is concentrated on progeria, but we are working on all sorts of initiatives. Milt, you have got to come up and see my lab."

Alex continued, "Wormer here has been useful in a different experiment—chemically induced genetic manipulation. Most genes found in nematodes are also found in humans. Wormer has fewer than 20,000 genes and fewer than 1,000 cells, and they are transparent. Under a microscope you see Wormer's parts as they respond to our experiments. Old Wormer won't mind if you take a look. And I mean *old* Wormer. He is at the end of a life cycle of six weeks—twice as long as normal and he has had plenty to eat." Alex set a home lab microscope on the table. He separated a sample the size of a pencil eraser and placed it on a slide, which he slid under the viewing portal.

Melanie went first. "I can detect motion."

Alex responded, "Yes, Melanie, it is a writhing mass of protein." Others followed.

Betsy raised her half-glass of wine, knelt down at eye level to the mess on her bridge table and said, "I'm hungry. Here's to you, Wormer von Braun." With one motion she raked up the nematodes and stuffed them in her mouth. She chugged the contents of her wine glass and after a big swallow said, "OK, whose deal?"

CHAPTER THIRTEEN

"Mary, next Wednesday on my afternoon off I want to visit Alex Morton in his Aging Institute laboratory."

Mary turned to Doc with an incredulous expression. She said, "Milt, you never take Wednesdays off. I have a full schedule of patients for you next Wednesday."

Doc was unshaken. He declared, "Mary, I'll work here through the lunch hour and at about two o'clock I'll want to go over to Rosenbaum. I'll see a few patients over there and then I'll go to the institute. I promised Alex."

The following Wednesday at 3:45 p.m. Doc exited the elevator on the sixth floor and proceeded down the hall to the Institute on Aging. Above the sign that read, "Rosenbaum Hospital Institute on Aging," there was a logo of a doctor that looked somewhat like Alex tilting a light-blue sand timer. There was some purple sand at the bottom and a lot of purple sand in the top section. The bottom of the sign read, "Established 1973 through the gracious gift of the Logan Howell family."

Doc identified himself to the receptionist. Less than five minutes later the door to the laboratory opened and Alex bounded out to vigorously shake Doc's hand. Alex said, "I've been visited by residents, fellows, equipment sellers, hospital administrators, family members, and curiosity-seekers. I have entertained mice, worms, monkeys, and fish, but this is the first time since we opened this lab two years ago that I have a chance to show it off to a close friend. Come on in, Milty. You're going to need to wear these." Alex reached for a pair of safety glasses. "That's lab protocol."

When they entered the laboratory, Alex spied someone leaning over a microscope and beckoned, "Hey Azi, come on over here. I want you to meet somebody. Milt, this is Azayiz Dansinghani, an M.D. and a brilliant biologist. He comes to us from Pakistan with an intermediate stop at Harvard Medical School. Azi, this is my good friend Milt Adams. Most people call him Doc."

Azi looked up from his microscope and shook Doc's hand. He said, "I know Doc Adams. He is my son Faraz's pediatrician."

"Of course," Doc said. "How is Faraz?"

"He's doing great, Doc. He's already in preschool."

"And how is Saima?"

"She is fine too. I'll tell her you asked about her."

Alex said, "Azi was a fellow at Indiana University. They've loaned him to us for a year to assist us on a critical progeria project. He was too valuable to release, so we hired him at the institute. I'll tell you about it later. Let me show you around."

Just to the left as the men entered the laboratory stood three cylindrical containers. Doc stood on his toes to peer over the top. Alex pointed to them and said, "These containers are kept at -80 degrees Celsius and are used to freeze tissues and cell samples in liquid nitrogen. At this temperature, cells can be frozen and, when they are carefully thawed out, they are completely viable. We store our nematodes in here—extraordinary creatures. They exhibit no ill-effects from that cryogenic environment.

Doc observed, "Alex, why so large? I could stuff my mother-in-law in one of those."

"Yes, we have the capacity to preserve larger species, including our rhesus macaques."

We can also store tissues in a substance that is similar to formaldehyde. This fixes the tissues and allows us to take our time to analyze them. In addition, look at this. Here are tissues embedded in a wax that also preserves them. There are all kinds of ways for us to deal with tissues and cell samples. The method we use depends upon the type of sample and how soon we want to begin our investigation."

The two doctors rounded a corner. "Here is where we begin that investigation. We've stored cells in this incubator that maintains optimal temperature, humidity, and other conditions, such as the CO_2 and oxygen content of the atmosphere inside." Doc shaded his eyes and peered inside. "At the bottom of those flasks you can see cells are growing in a solution. Watch your head, Milty. This air-flow hood shields the area from airborne fungus and other contaminants, even if you were to penetrate this air barrier with your gloved hands and sterilized tools. Basically, we keep the bad air from getting in while we manipulate the cells in this sterile environment.

Along this corridor we installed DNA, hematology, and blood gas analyzers. This immunoassay analyzer identifies and detects the concentration of specific substances in a sample. Here is the histology and pathology equipment that we use to prepare and examine tissues. These processors produce thin tissue slices and prepare the samples for study.

On this bench in the corner are a number of microscopes, but not the kind you might find in your medical school laboratory. These are equipped with modern fluorescent illumination. They allow us to engage in total internal reflection fluorescence. This is a cutting-edge optical technique that excites the fluorophores in a fragile axial region to visualize the cellular events occurring close to the cell surface. If you don't understand all this or how it works, it makes no difference. I spent one afternoon studying this technology until I had it down pat. I went to sleep that night and when I woke up the next morning, I didn't understand any of it. I do know, in this way, we can mark certain cells with a probe that imparts a fluorescent glow that is picked up by these special electron microscopes. They are delicate instruments. That's why we keep them separate and way over here in a corner. The technique has made it easier to understand the mechanism and function of cellular components. We can use these microscopes to visualize a single molecule. Milty, take a look under this microscope. You'll see what I'm talking about."

Doc was no stranger to a microscope, but he had never been treated to fluorescent illumination. He readily accepted the invitation. As Doc began to concentrate, Alex said to him, "Look carefully and you'll spot the fluorescent delineation."

Doc thought, "I would have enjoyed the life of a research scientist."

Alex and Doc proceeded down a hall with work benches and the usual array of hardware and supplies, including microscopes, shelves of Petri dishes, and tools, ranging from ordinary and expected, to shapes and sizes that were confounding to a general-practice pediatrician. On the shelves were beakers, Bunsen burners, evaporating dishes, and test tubes. Doc caught some movement out of his left eye. He looked down and saw four cages of mice. In one cage the mice were a striking white.

Alex said, "We call the albino mice BALB/c. They were reliably bred for experimentation. The brown ones have had their immunity removed. If we were to take them out of this enclosed special environment, they would die, whereas the white ones would live."

Just down from the mice cages were three fish tanks. Two of the tanks were filled with dozens of goldfish. The third tank appeared to be empty. Alex pointed to the tanks, "This experiment is underway for our students to confirm we can double the life span of fish by lowering their body temperature. Put on these gloves and put the finger of your left hand in the first tank and a finger of your right hand in the second tank." Doc did as instructed and noticed the marked temperature differential.

Alex warned, "Do not put either hand in the third tank. Put your gloves in this waste receptacle."

When Doc looked closely at the third tank, he saw one fish. It was the color of milk chocolate. It was motionless in the corner of the tank, easily missed at a first glance but for a few red markings visible on its underbelly. Alex dipped into the control tank with a cup and captured one of the goldfish. He said, "We have our own disposal unit for this experiment." He emptied the cup in the third tank with a purposeful splash. Doc watched as the two fish started at opposite ends of the tank. In a short while, the original occupant swam out of its corner. Doc could see the protruding jawbone with a row of razor-edged teeth on the top and bottom.

Doc looked up and said, "Alex, that's a piranha."

"Yes, Doc, its name is Simon."

For two minutes in what appeared to be an elaborate choreographed tango the two fish swam the tank from end to end. Then, in a lightning-fast strike the piranha swam behind the goldfish and devoured it. Ten seconds later Simon's powerful jaws had stripped the goldfish bare. Its skeleton drifted lazily to the bottom of the tank.

Doc said, "Wouldn't it be easier to just feed the goldfish to Betsy?" Alex laughed and said, "Sometimes I would like to invite the Jester in for a swim. He can be meddlesome."

Doc rarely offered unsolicited advice. He said, "The Jester has a rare intellect and an intense curiosity. Please forgive him. He doesn't mean to be meddlesome."

Alex turned to a closed door that bore a sign illuminated in bright red that said, "Experiment in Process—Radioactive—BEWARE."

He said, "This is our radioactive lab and it looks like we can't go in there at this time. Radioactivity is important in many biological lab analyses. Perhaps we'll explore that room another day."

Alex opened the next door. It was marked, "PRIVATE." They entered a room with an oak desk and two matching chairs facing a plush sofa, all resting on light green carpet. Awards and degrees were displayed on the wall behind the desk. Milt stepped over to the opposite wall to appreciate the art above the sofa. He read, "Monet" in the bottom right corner. He let out a whistle. "Is that real?"

Alex shrugged his shoulders. "Not my choice. It was a birthday gift to Betsy from Logan. She let me hang it in here until she finds a place to put it. You wouldn't want this. Why, the insurance premium on the painting would break us both."

Doc looked at the opposite wall. "What's that?"

Alex rolled his eyes. "That is an Indianapolis Racers hockey stick autographed by Logan himself. It came with the Monet."

Alex motioned to Doc, "Milty, please sit down." Alex took two small beakers from the shelf and filled them with ice from a refrigerator inside one of the cabinets. He opened another cabinet and brought out a fifth of Chivas Regal. "Water or straight-up, Milty?"

Milt raised his hands and said, "Alex, you know I don't drink very much. Add a little water in there and I'll sip it. I didn't know you imbibed, Alex."

"Only after hours. But your visit is a special occasion. Milt, research is a circuitous road. It requires patience and tolerance for failure. It's depressing to put time and effort into something and have nothing to show for it. Chivas softens the blow once in a while."

The men sat down, and Alex began, "Again, I'd like to welcome you to my aerie. I've been anxious to tell you about the preliminary results of our experiments to help Jimmy and other progeria patients. We've been at this for about two years and I can report some success so far and we did it right here in this lab that you've just toured.

"We could use more sophisticated equipment, but we have already spent all of Logan's donation. The larger labs in major research institutes are kind enough to accord access to Rosenbaum scientists, and we do OK here with what we've got. Our facilities are sufficient for us to run our "lone wolf" investigation.

"Milty, you told us, what seems like centuries ago, progeria has been around for more than fifty years. In fact, it was first diagnosed in the late 1800s, almost 100 years ago. It has affected so few people that nobody but some distraught and desperate family members seemed to care. Big Pharma can't make any money on it. These companies aren't going to create drugs they can't sell. Scientists can overcome the enormous challenges of developing vaccines that rescue humanity, for example, Jonas Salk and his team, but scientists make choices. And those who could probably solve the problem have undertaken more lucrative and romantic pursuits. Can you blame them? Can you expect them to devote their careers to save a few dozen children? Milty, you are my closest friend. I need your advice. Do you think scientists have an obligation without any additional justification, to investigate diseases that affect only an infinitesimal few? Do I? In this lab, by coincidence of your referring Jimmy to me, I have accepted this responsibility. Should I have? It's not about money. Betsy's father, Logan, has taken care of all of that. Is it about career opportunity or is it about creating a breakthrough that will save the lives of somebody's children? I just have second thoughts. Progeria is a long-shot, but with the help of Azi and some of the other folks around here, we are destined to achieve victory. Without us, that boy is doomed."

CHAPTER FOURTEEN

On a sunny July afternoon in Karachi, two young Pakistanis entered Mohammad's coffee shop on Nakhlisan Street, just off of Napier Road. Napier was considered the northern boundary of the red-light district of Karachi in the 1960s. Motorcycles, pedestrians, bicycles, buses, taxis, and vans all wrestled for six narrow lanes. At 1:30, the two young men were shown to a table. The waiter, Hasan, told the police officer he knew exactly what time it was. It was his table. The young men were dressed in Western garb. One wore a T-shirt with the logo of the British soccer team Tranmere Rovers. The other wore a New York Giants baseball cap. They unshouldered their backpacks, glanced at the menus and ordered black coffee with cinnamon.

Most of the tables in Mohammad's coffee shop were full on this Thursday afternoon. There was little room on the patio as well. Mohammad's boasted a diverse mixture of locals, businessmen and tourists from the Hotel Srinager across the street. Many of the patrons were under thirty, which accounted for the brisk business in hashish. Heroin and other nefarious drugs were not sold at the coffee shop, by order of Mohammad. The drug cartels complied with the restriction. There were plenty of coffee shops and other venues in which to ply their trade. Still, the all-powerful Pakistani and Afghani drug lords harbored resentment.

After forty-five minutes, the two young men left ten rupees on the table, shouldered their backpacks and went through the side door to the back-hall stairway. There were two apartments on the second floor, generally rented by the day. Keys were available for cash payment at the bar. The two young men tiptoed to the third floor, which housed the offices of *Umeed*, a local weekly newspaper founded by Shafi Dansinghani and his partner Usif Shahzad. *Umeed*, meaning "hope" in Urdu, was the name chosen for their publication. It reflected the optimism of the two journalists.

For all its three years, *Umeed* managed to stay just within the fringe of tolerated speech in Karachi. The partners had received clandestine warnings from drug lords and city hall just two months ago, in May, after publishing "Do You Remember, a Lamentable History of Karachi." The essay ended with the lines:

Do you remember when Karachi was safe to stroll through the park in the evening? Do you remember when our children could play on the sidewalks without a bodyguard? Do you remember when coffee was the primary product sold at a coffeehouse? Do you remember when city hall was responsible to its citizens?

In its last edition, *Umeed* published a cartoon that depicted the mayor of Karachi smoking a cigar lit by unsavory-looking Afghanis. The mayor's foot was on the neck of citizens of Karachi, while his hand was accepting money from a Pakistani drug seller.

The young men paused on the staircase in front of the door leading to the third floor to unpack and assemble Russian Kalashnikov automatic rifles, affixed with silencers. There was no need for masks. The men were under orders to eliminate all *Umeed* personnel. They re-shouldered their backpacks, walked down the hall and began a search of each office. The individual offices were empty. In one room, ten men and women sat around a conference table strewn with papers. The two young men blocked the door. Shafi Dansinghani's partner, Usif Shahzad, had less than ten seconds to stand and plead for their lives. He was shot first. Both assailants shot the woman at the head of the table. Then one of the young men proceeded to the left and the other to the right blasting at each occupant. A gurgling noise was detected from under the table. One of the youths bent to his knees to peer at a man sitting up still holding a red pencil and trying to breathe through a hole in his neck. In seconds, the youth fired three quick bursts. The man dropped his pencil and fell over in slow motion. The gurgling ceased.

When the slaughter was completed, the young men took from their backpacks explosive devices crammed with volatile compounds of ammonium nitrate and began planting them throughout the suite. In one of the rooms a man caught sight of a small girl hiding under a desk.

"What is your name?"

"Yushfa."

He motioned to her with his rifle. Yushfa crawled out from under the desk with eyes wide with fear. She straightened her summer dress. The man raised his gun and aimed it directly at her heart. She was frozen but managed a weak smile. The man motioned with his weapon for her to leave the room. Earlier that day she and her mother had taken the bus for three kilometers to the office, where her mother had promised an important duty for her. She had chosen her favorite dress, the pink one with yellow and white jasmine designs. Just an hour before, mother and daughter had enjoyed a quiet lunch at Sabri Chai and Biscuits. Yushfa ran to the conference room and saw her mother splayed across her chair motionless and bleeding from multiple wounds in her chest. She cast a panicked eye on the scene. It was quiet— almost peaceful. As she turned to run, she slipped on the blood flowing in crisscrossing rivers of autumn red. Yushfa ran down the stairs to the first floor and bolted out the back door. She ran screaming down the sidewalk of Napier Street and across Zanzana Park. She stopped running when she reached home. She could not stop crying.

The two men set off the timed charges and trotted down the stairs and out the back door to a waiting black sedan. They were more than two blocks away when the neighborhood was jolted by loud claps, like thunder, and funnels of smoke. As the three-story building crashed within itself, it encompassed the entire block with volcanic belching, simmering, and frightening noise. After too many minutes, firemen on the scene blocked off the streets and began to protect nearby buildings from the menacing flames. Patrons escaping the Hotel Srinager across the street were met with a wall of spray as the firemen began to win the battle to save the hotel. The tobacconist on the corner did not fare as well. His store burst into flames. The odor of roasted tobacco mixed with the coffee shop blends and the flesh of burning victims. Ambulances arrived and ferried injured pedestrians to the hospital. The coffee shop, the two second-floor apartments and the third floor yielded no survivors. The waiter, Hasan, survived only because he was outside clearing tables on the patio.

Shafi's brother, Sikandar Dansinghani, ran to the scene. Sikandar was the owner of three coffee shops, one of which was located two blocks from the disaster area. Sikandar did not hide from his family that he had business relationships with the drug cartels, for which he was handsomely compensated. He often bragged to his brother Shafi, "As they say in America, 'I am playing some ball' with these guys."

When Sikandar saw that nobody in the building had survived, he sped on his motorcycle to his brother's apartment. He burst into the home and cried, "Where is Jasmine?" She hurried to the door. Sikandar put his hands on her shoulders and cried, "Jasmine, your husband has died in a terrible explosion." Sikandar felt a tap on the shoulder. He looked around. Shafi said, "Sikandar, I'm right here."

After a tearful embrace, Shafi explained, "I came home early. Don't you remember? It's Azi's birthday. He is twenty-one today."

Sikandar said, "This disaster is a means for the drug cartel to silence the newspaper and to send a message to everyone that the drug gangs are in control of Karachi. I am certain that city hall is on the drug payroll and consented to the despicable mission.

When they learn that you escaped, your life will not be worth one rupee. You need to leave as soon as possible. Gather your family, pack your valuable belongings. Don't leave your house. I'll be back at ten."

As soon as Sikandar left, Azi slipped out the back door. He crept down the alley and stayed in the shadows. Ten minutes later he was in a safe and quiet apartment in the arms of his love, Saima. She had heard about the explosion. Everyone had. She held Azi. "I was afraid you could not come." His hand slid under her shirt, as she continued their conversation.

"I was looking forward to giving you something special for your birthday."

He gasped, "I remember what you promised."

Saima removed her red scarf and threw it over her left shoulder. She said, "Happy birthday, dear Azi."

Azi stroked her long black hair until she was finished.

Azi shared his family's plans to evacuate Karachi.

Saima protested, "My dearest Azi, you were at the top of your class in Metric and in Intercom. You're supposed to begin Dow Medical School in two months. Please stay. These evil people aren't after you."

Azi replied, "I belong with my family, wherever we must go."

Saima sobbed, "Promise me you will never lose sight of your goal. You will make a fine doctor. If you cannot return to Karachi, make your way to America and send for me. I love you, Azi. Now you must leave."

Azi picked up Saima's scarf and put it around her neck. He held her face in his hands and looked deeply in her eyes. They were a dusky electric green. "You are lovely, Saima, and special to me." He placed a gentle kiss on her lips. Then he was gone.

CHAPTER FIFTEEN

Azi retraced his steps and sneaked in his back door at 9:45, in time to answer the soft knock at the door at precisely 10:00. Sikandar entered without a word, withdrew a map from his valise and spread it out on the kitchen table. Shafi and Azi leaned over as Sikandar spoke. "Your best chance of escape is India. As you know, we reside in a bad neighborhood." Sikandar took his pencil and pointed first at Afghanistan. "You can't go here. Those people are desperate to cross into Pakistan." He pointed to Iran. "I need not say anything about this option." He then said, "China is too far to the north. India is our only alternative, and I have decided that we will guide you up north and then across the Thar Desert."

Shafi protested, "Why do we need to brave the dangers of the Thar when India is just a few hours by sea? We could make port in Porbandor."

Sikandar had considered that route. He said, "This would be impossible." He pointed to the Arabian Sea and said, "One, Somali pirates control this area. You and your family would be enslaved before your boat reached the end of the jetty. Two, the Afghani drug cartel has established dominion over the sea route along the coast. Wouldn't they love to finish off the only threat they missed this morning? Three, there are Pakistani gun boats who might mistake you for any enemy of Pakistan. And four, who knows what would await you in Indian waters before you make port in Porbandor?"

"Your best bet is for me to drive you through the night to Sukkur, a distance of approximately four hundred kilometers. Here." Sikandar traced the route on the map. "Before we leave tonight, we will have secured you a safe house there. We will arrange a van for tomorrow night from Sukkur across the border with India and deliver you to Bikaner." As he spoke, he drew a light line from Karachi to Sukkur to Bikaner. "The border is porous. You should have no problems with Indian authorities." He continued the line as he said, "You will take a train to New Delhi and contact your cousins here." He jammed his pencil on the map in triumph. He then turned to Jasmine and said, "Pack food for the journey. It will be too dangerous to stop."

The Dansinghani family, Shafi, his wife, Jasmine, Azayiz, and his sixteen-year-old sister, Laila, dressed for the journey. Laila wore a young boy's robe on the advice of her mother, who felt her daughter would be safer at the border as a male. Regardless of garb, Laila was unmistakable as a girl on the cusp of womanhood whose figure refused to be restrained by a boy's cloak. Her eyes were the color of the finest jade, and her smile, an offer of friendship hard to refuse.

Sikandar gave his brother, Shafi, an envelope stuffed with American currency, four $100 bills and five $20 bills. He also handed him a neatly folded paper containing hand-printed addresses and phone numbers of their cousins in New Delhi.

Sikandar handed Azi a Pakistani TT-30 pistol. Azi protested, "I've never fired a pistol." His uncle laughed, "It's very simple, you just point like a camera and shoot." Azi slipped it inside his breast pocket.

It was 11:00 on a moonless night when the family climbed in Sikandar's van and proceeded through the streets of Karachi, then due north. They reached Sukkur at dawn.

They disembarked from the van and hugged their goodbyes. Azi watched Shafi hug his brother Sikandar, as they exchanged a few soft words. Sikandar spoke to Azi. "Azayiz, you are twenty-one. You are a man. With the help of Allah, take care of your mother and father and your sister, Laila."

"I vow to do that, Uncle Sikandar. Yes, it will be so."

The safe house was a two-room hut occupied by a pleasant woman bent by years of manual labor. She met them at her front door with the greeting, "Salaam, I am Aisha." She served them a light meal and beckoned them to the mats that were strewn about the floor.

The next evening at 10:00, after each received a hug from Aisha, the family walked a block south of the safe house. Three men carrying machine guns and dressed in white robes escorted them to an empty van. The tallest of the three wore a red bandana. He demanded the agreed-upon payment in advance, $100 per passenger in American currency. He stuffed the bills inside his robe. The one they referred to as Arsalan sat in the driver's seat. Azi was tired. The mats on the floor had allowed for only a few hours of fitful sleep. He wandered to the back seats, found a comfortable position and fell asleep before Arsalan started the van.

The van had bumped along for hours when Azi was awakened by a woman's screams. It was his sister. He knew it. He also noticed the van was not moving. The rat-a-tat of assault weapons brought him to full alert. Azi sat up and peered out the window, but he couldn't see anything more than shadows in the desert darkness. He sneaked around behind the van, where he saw two of the men kneeling over his mother and father savagely searching their pockets and ripping their clothing for anything of value. Azi crept behind the man with the red bandana who was on his knees over his father, placed the pistol at the back of the man's head and pulled the trigger. Blood burst from his forehead and splattered over Shafi's body. The second man raised up and dived for his weapon. Azi shot him in his mid-section. He went down and began to crawl toward his rifle. Azi, in an unexplained state of calm, walked over and fired two more shots into the man's head. He put his new pistol back in his breast pocket and picked up one of the assault rifles.

He looked toward the direction of the screams at the top of a sand dune. They had ceased. He noticed a shape moving toward him down the hill. Azi knelt into the darkness and lifted the assault rifle. When the shape was within twenty yards, it took human form. It was the driver, Arsalan. Azi aimed the weapon and let it rip three rounds, two of which caught the man in his chest. The man fell and rolled to the bottom of the sand dune at Azi's feet. Azi pumped three more rounds into the dying man. He dropped the rifle and ran to his sister at the top of the sand dune. She was naked from the waist down. Her throat had been gashed. Her once dazzling green eyes were lifeless. Azi screamed and wailed. He ran down to the bloody scene below and rifled through the robe of his father's killer. He pocketed the contents, which included the American currency Shafi had given him that evening. He leapt into the van and sped east. Azi didn't stop screaming for the next two hours, until the bus sputtered, popped and, spewing black steam, stopped in the middle of the sandy road.

Azi allowed himself no time to think. He shouldered a few belongings and resumed his journey east on foot. Azi carried no weight on his six-foot frame. In elementary school he was teased by classmates, who said if Azi turned just so, they could see right through him. At twenty-one he weighed a scant 140 pounds. There was no word for lanky in Urdu.

Azi had no idea how far he was from Bikaner. He could see a few hundred yards by the dawn's light. After five hours of plodding in the deafening desert silence, he collapsed in the blazing morning sun at the edge of a small village. Azi was not the first poor soul to wander across the Thar. Some made it. Many did not. He woke two hours later in a village tent. When he sat up, two men in light brown desert robes offered him many cups of a liquid he could not identify. Azi's eyes darted in fear.

The man with a flowing white beard said in Hindi, "Assalamu Alaikum, "I am Basheer."

Azi blurted out in Pakistani-accented Urdu, "I am a refugee from Pakistan. My life is in danger. I escaped across the border last night through the Great Indian Desert. I seek sanctuary. I must reach the train station in Bikaner. People who meet me there will pay you when we arrive. Please help me."

The other man patted Azi on the shoulder and answered in Urdu, "Bikaner is twelve kilometers east. I am going to Bikaner to visit my daughter after the noonday sun. Rest now. You may go with me."

Azi replied, "Allah apko iska ajr de" and fell back down on his cot. He was awakened from a deep sleep at 4:00 in the afternoon with some naan and a glass of water.

"We go now."

Azi emerged from the tent, blinked his eyes from the afternoon sun and followed the villager down the path. He looked in all directions, but could discern nothing more than an undulating deathless expanse of sand. Within twenty yards of the tent that had been his respite for most of the day, he saw three palm trees in a small grove and a wire fence that protected four goats from the jackals and the white desert foxes of the Thar. There was also a camel tied to one of the fence posts. The camel was adorned with a blanket of green and red geometric designs. The colors, once rich and vibrant, had long ago fallen victim to the unsparing rays of the desert sun.

His new friend clasped him on the shoulder and said, "I am Mousa, let me help you mount my camel." Azi cried softly to himself the entire ride.

Azi and Mousa dismounted at the Bikaner train station. Azi offered $20 in American currency to Mousa, who protested. Azi finally took two $20 bills and gently put them in Mousa's pocket. Mousa bowed his head and said, "Khuda hafiz" as the men parted.

Azi stood in line for ten minutes for his chance to make a call from the train station pay telephone. He spoke with his cousin at the second number on the list Sikandar had provided and was assured family would meet him in New Delhi. He purchased a ticket with rupees he had found in the dead man's pocket and left that evening on the overnight train.

After a six-hour ride, a bath, a meal, and a fitful sleep, Azi was ready to tell his story and to ask his relatives to assist in his journey. He had decided that he wanted to live in the United States of America.

CHAPTER SIXTEEN

Alex and Azi sat underneath the Monet in Alex's private office for their weekly Friday afternoon meeting. Their self-invited guest was Marty Colson, who had postponed his golf game that spring day. He had left his blue suit and paisley tie in the closet and was sporting snappy green slacks and a short-sleeved shirt with a praying mantis logo. He hoped to complete his business in time for a 3:45 tee time. The hospital administrator wanted a progress report on lab experiments. It was more than a curiosity. Colson was under the latest assault by Micah Davis and some of his cronies. Colson referred to him as, "that Bozo in the bobbing bow tie."

Alex unhooked the Racer hockey stick and began to swing it. "Gentlemen, we are on a noble quest. We are trying to arrest, no, we are *trying* to cure, progeria. We are squarely focused on this quest. We will find the key."

Azi was game. He nodded his head in agreement and smiled. Azi had picked up most of the nuances in his second language. He thought, "Sometimes, Alex, your exhilaration can be trying."

Alex continued, "Marty, to summarize for you, so far, no breakthrough, but we have developed our strategy to identify the gene causing all this trouble. But let's start at the end result and work backward. The nuclear membrane in each of Jimmy Higgins' cells is malformed, which over time damages the structure and function of the nucleus, causing the cells to die prematurely. That is the essence of progeria.

"So, what is causing the nuclear membrane to be malformed? It is a stunted form of lamin A, a protein that is faulty to the extent that it cannot be processed correctly within the cell. We sometimes refer to the abnormal lamin A as 'progerin.' Working backward from the abnormal lamin A, we know that a mutated gene is giving the wrong instructions to the lamin A protein. The secret would be to find that mutated gene and replace it.

Colson glanced at his watch and said, "I think I understand this. The Higgins boy has a bad gene that causes his cells to die early."

Alex nodded. "That is a gross oversimplification, Marty, but you have captured the essence of the problem. Let me go on.

"How do we locate the gene that causes the faulty lamin A? We extract the lamin A from the compromised nuclear membrane, and we compare that to the normal lamin A to pinpoint the mutated gene that codes for the defective lamin A. We do that through gel electrophoresis. We refer to that process as 'running the gel.'

"Think of the chromosomes as a long highway made out of DNA. We break the long highway into segments using enzymes, and we stain the segments so that they will show up under fluorescent microscopes. We then compare normal and progeria segments side by side in a slide of gelatin. We run a current through the gelatin and observe whether the snippets move differently through the gel. If so, we have our culprit. If not, we continue to compare additional DNA segments along that highway."

Azi was as bright as Alex and more impatient. "OK Alex, we all know progeria must be solved at the molecular level. We have been at it six months. We've collected our tissue samples. We have ample specimens from Jimmy Higgins, and we can procure more. We have samples from Jonesy, the Mason City kid, and the two others who are planning to visit Disneyland with Jimmy. Dr. Yosso sends fresh supplies of foreskin. We can then compare our progeria samples with normal unadulterated tissues. As long as people have baby boys, we'll have foreskin."

Azi continued, "We precipitated the DNA in these tissues by ridding them of the proteins and sugars and we have added enzymes to the goop to make it more manageable for analysis." We are 'running the gel' and moving down the chromosome highway. When we analyzed and compared the genes from the progerians, we detected slight differences. That is what we expected. After all, we are all different individuals. The trick is to discover the difference or differences between the progerian gene and the gene from the normal tissues." Azi turned to face Colson. "Like Alex said, after we isolate that difference, we will extract that segment from the gel. When we chemically identify and isolate the DNA from that segment, we will have found Gene P, the terrorist gene that has disrupted the cells in our progeria patients."

Colson stopped Azi's recitation, "You haven't found the 'mean gene,' but you have developed a methodology."

Alex took up the narrative. "OK, here's the problem: Thousands of genes lie hidden in each of the chromosomes that dot the nucleus of every cell. In order to isolate Gene P, we may have to make as many as 50,000 comparisons. How many genes have we compared so far?"

Azi checked his lab notes. "We have made 1,000 uneventful comparisons, all in chromosome one."

Alex was quick with his mental calculation. "OK, with colossal bad luck we have 49,000 more to do. At a rate of 1,000 per six months, we have to spend another twenty-four and a half years. How much time do you have to spend with us, Azi?"

Azi didn't answer that question. Marty broke in, "Indiana University Hospital and some of the finest research institutions in the country have already inquired about Azi."

Azi resumed, "We're scientists. We are intuitive here. Based upon recent accounts of gene investigation in the literature and our own tentative conclusions from what we have gathered so far, we can make educated guesses where Gene P is not located on the chromosomes. We can narrow down the next phase to richer opportunities, maybe 2,500 comparisons. I'll check with colleagues at Columbia who are engaged in research at the cellular level. They may have some insights on where we should not look. Our equipment will facilitate two more skilled technicians. The Jester is competent. He'd like a try when his practice allows." Alex groaned.

This time Azi did the math. "If our educated guesses are correct and our comparison rate is doubled, we can find Gene P before the end of the year."

Alex said to himself, "Hang on, Jimmy, the cavalry is on its way."

Marty interjected, "It can't be that simple. The disease has been killing children for a century and you're going to vanquish it within the year?"

Alex answered, "Even if we isolate Gene P, there are more questions to ask. Finding the cause is not equivalent to finding the cure, and we haven't found the cause. We only think we can do that."

Azi had succumbed to Alex's exhilaration. He broke in, "No, we're sure we can do that. It is just a matter of patience."

Alex offered Marty and Azi a glass of scotch. They clinked and drained their glasses.

******

Six months later, Alex entered the lab at 10:00 on a Monday morning rubbing his hands and pounding his shoulders to combat the November chill. Azi grabbed him before he could unzip his jacket. Alex followed Azi to the "fluorescent area."

Azi beckoned Alex to the work bench and said, "Have a look at the second electron microscope."

Alex remembered his heart rate at graduation when the dean first addressed him as "Doctor." It was beating that fast again. Alex bent to the eyepiece. "What am I seeing, Azi?"

"You are seeing the devastation wrought by that mean and terrible Gene P. We found it on chromosome one. We know the normal iteration of that gene directs the production of the protein that holds the nucleus of the cell together, but look at the protein result in the diseased cell. At the direction of this mutated gene, the cell is producing progerin, the lamin A protein causing the nucleus to be unstable, leading to its premature aging and death.

"What you are seeing, Alex, is progeria."

CHAPTER SEVENTEEN

"Shall we notify Marty?" It was Azi's first question at the next Friday afternoon meeting.

Alex was firm. "No, Azi. We have made a remarkable discovery but as we have said, 'no cure.' We have identified and isolated Gene P. Alex pumped his fist as he said, "Azi, let's harvest cells from the Higgins samples and place them in our incubator. We will need to perform some confirmations before we take further steps." Alex began to pace the floor.

"There are 100 trillion cells in the human body. Jimmy will not benefit from our discovery until we can access them all and replace Gene P. It may take centuries to solve the riddle and help that boy. Azi, if we agree to skip lunch, maybe we can get this done a little quicker."

Azi laughed. "In Urdu we say, 'Aasmaan say gira khajoor mein atka.' It means 'Get out of one trouble but fall into another one.'"

Alex said, "We say, 'Go from the frying pan into the fire.'"

Alex continued, "The cell is like an exclusive party to which we have not been invited. There are bouncers at the gate who will not let us crash. We have to hoodwink the bouncers and slip through the gate."

"Hoodwink?"

"Bamboozle."

"Bamboozle?"

"Azi, we have to trick the gatekeepers and sneak our way through the plasma membrane."

Two days later, Azi placed a file on Alex's desk. It was labeled, "Trojan Horse."

The first document in the file was a short memo from Azi: *An Indiana biopharmaceutical company is developing target-small-molecule drug conjugates for personalized therapy. The company's discoveries actively target receptors that are over-expressed in diseased cells. Alex, in words that Marty will understand, cancer cells replicate wildly and, like neonatal cells, greedily consume the vitamin folate, a requirement for cell division. Because some cancers need so much folate, they absorb it using receptors unique to those cancers. This company's novel approach is to target those receptors with folate and lace the folate with their Trojan horse, cancer-fighting drugs many times more potent than tolerated by normal cells under customary delivery systems, and administer those drugs more frequently over longer periods of time. The goal is to knock out the cancer without poisoning normal cells.* Alex's mind was racing to determine how that theory would be applicable to progeria research. He sat up straight, put his palm on his forehead and said, "We're not trying to solve cancer here, we're talking about delivery systems." He turned to the next page.

Azi continued with a new memo: *Preliminary experience has shown that this company has solved the problem of sneaking its drug past the bouncers at the cell gates. If we concentrate our next phase on what substances the cells would allow to enter and lace those compounds with the normal Gene P, the human body would do the rest and sow that seed to all 100 trillion cells. If it works for folate, it could work for us.*

Alex turned to the next page. Azi concluded: *Folate will not work. What we need to look for is the organism that doesn't just seek out special receptors in cancer cells and neonatal cells, but one that will crash into every cell. When we isolate that organism, we can lace it with our normal Gene P and watch a miracle occur in front of our noses.*

Alex closed the file. He put his elbows on top of the file and clasped his face with his hands, resting his chin in his palms. He reflected on Azi. Here was this young man who once told him a story about his escape from Karachi so harrowing that Alex did not know whether to believe it. One day when Saima stopped by to bring Azi's lunch, Alex held the door open for her and said, "Saima, how did you end up with Azi?"

Saima had replied, "His family fled Pakistan in order to avoid some very bad people. He made it to America, where we live our lives in safety and comfort, but my dear Azi is still traumatized by the events of his escape. He has nightmares. I tell him he needs a therapist, but he won't listen. Do you know he still carries a loaded pistol his uncle gave him? That loaded gun makes me nervous. He sent for me and I know he loves me, but he thinks I boss him around too much. I think it's good for him."

Alex smiled at the thought of his reply. "Saima, you have become the perfect American wife."

The next Friday afternoon session stretched well into the evening. The two scientists discussed the dilemma over a wide range of disciplines. They tossed around the theory of delivering Gene P by utilizing stem cells. They discussed the efficacy of combining Gene P with a safe vaccine for another disease, like polio or the mumps. They discussed removing Gene P altogether and injecting a formulated protein every day like insulin for diabetes. The discussions were stimulating, but led nowhere.

Azi stood up to leave. He put on a surgical mask.

Alex asked, "What's on your mask? Are you operating at the hospital during this late hour?"

"That face on my mask is Iskander Mirza, first president of Pakistan. My uncle, Sikandar, sent me a box of these from Karachi, where they are dealing with a wave of ailments. I brought a mask with me today because there is a rumor of an outbreak of some virus on the third floor. I know Rosenbaum is noted as a clean hospital, but I decided to wear the mask in the halls just to be safe." Azi left the private office.

Alex jumped from the sofa and raced to the door. He caught Azi in the waiting room, whirled him around and said, "Did you say virus?"

Azi's mouth dropped open. He recovered and answered Alex. "Sure, a virus invades our cells and deposits its genetic material into the cell nucleus, and yes, it's theoretically possible to lace that virus with a normal Gene P, but in the fragile state of our progeria patient, these parasites will kill him before we can effect a cure. Alex, you are scaring me. The world is teeming with viruses. There are more viruses on earth than stars in the Milky Way. The war between humans and viruses is raging. Viruses kill more living things than any other type of predator, and you want to turn one loose on Jimmy?

"Yes, Azi, we do live in a world of abundant viruses, but we couldn't live without them. A virus is a parasite, but sometimes that relationship can be just as critical to the host as it is to the visitor."

"But Jimmy would be a vulnerable host. With his weakened system and existing respiratory stress and cardiac disease, he will be at higher risk of developing severe illness from the virus."

Alex raised both hands, palms out. "Hold it, Azi. In a hospital setting with round-the-clock care we should be able to win these battles. A virus is nothing more than a bit of DNA inside a protein coat. It has an infectious power. Burrowing into cells is second nature to it. I propose we harness our enemy and use a viral vector as a carrier to transport our genetic correction. It's our Trojan horse! Perhaps there is a virus or a number of viruses that can enter a cell, yet not capitalize on the vulnerability of the patient. Let's at least look in that direction."

They met again early the next morning. Alex clung to the virus concept. "Our first step will be to set up flasks of progeria tissue and methodically introduce common, less lethal viruses into the cell structure with its passenger, the normal Gene P. I'm referring to viruses that can cause cold or flu-like symptoms, fever, pink eye, and sore throat. Let's wait on the more deadly strains—acute bronchitis, pneumonia, and acute gastroenteritis, to name a few. The less dangerous viruses will dissipate in less than a week. Let's get copies of these and determine how effective they are at delivering the payload."

Within days a research team determined that adenoviruses, but only in their active and virulent form, penetrated the cells in the flasks and delivered the normal Gene P intact. Azi explained it to Alex, "The genus of adenoviruses has a unique spike that aids in the attachment to the host cell via the receptor on the surface of the cell. In our experiments, the normal Gene P dominated the offending gene and took its place. Think of this as the idiomatic expression, square peg and round hole. The defective gene is the square peg that does not fit well in the round hole of the nucleus membrane. The normal Gene P is the round peg and bonds perfectly, rendering the defective gene useless. The cell is then given instruction from Gene P to make the normal lamin A protein."

Azi studied the results at the work bench. He leaned back on his stool and shouted, "Zabardast!"

Alex and Azi set up the next experiment with the lab technicians. It was to determine the effect of various iterations of the less toxic adenovirus on the disease-resistant mice. The goal was to choose the adenovirus that was the most effective with the least toxicity. They monitored the mice over the next week. The mice were failing from a variety of diseases. Instructions were given to the technicians not to sacrifice the animals but to keep them alive until they tested healthy once more. Twelve BALB/c mice were subjected to the experiment. Ten survived the first two weeks.

Alex said, "Azi, if we had a few years we could determine how to strip the virus of the genes that allow it to reproduce. In that manner, once it gets into the cell and unloads Gene P, it would be unable to produce more copies of itself and would die away."

The scientists concluded that Jimmy would have the highest chance of survival with the virus that causes the common cold. That mouse was stepping lively.

Azi cautioned, "Alex, that strain can kill as well. Jimmy may run a high fever and suffer respiratory distress."

Alex said, "I know. I know, but let's go with it. It's our best shot."

The team was ready for step two. Over the next few weeks Higgins cells were assaulted with experiments. Azi brought Alex up to date. "Left to grow in their flasks, the Higgins cells' replication process proceeded at a slower than normal rate, sputtered, and ceased. Cell death ensued. When Gene P was extracted from healthy mice tissue, it died abruptly. In other experiments, hosts of enzymes were introduced to counteract the instructions of the defective Gene P, to no avail.

When copies of the normal Gene P from the foreskin tissue were introduced via the adenovirus vector, they dominated the activity to the exclusion of the defective gene. The cell, on instruction from the normal gene, began producing the protein to stabilize the nucleus and to perform in the manner for which it was designed. Cells began to replicate and show outward signs of normalcy."

Azi wasn't convinced. "Suppose Jimmy Higgins underwent this gene replacement therapy. In theory, if we could stave off the ill effects of the virus for, let's say, a week or two, we may effect a cure of Jimmy's progeria disease, but if we fail, Jimmy may die. Even if we combat the adenovirus, we still don't know for sure whether the delivery will work. Most new treatments, even those that have shown promise in the lab, are met with diminishing returns as they move up to more complex animals. They have almost no effect when tested in humans, who are genetically diverse. We have never even tried this with dogs, for example."

Alex was undeterred. "Azi, life is a risk. We cannot live risk-free even if we want to. As scientists, we manage risk. We balance risk. The bigger the payoff, the more risk we should tolerate. We have an opportunity not only to save Jimmy and his fellow sufferers, but to eradicate a disease. If we don't do anything, we know what the outcome will be. Jimmy will die, and soon. We've all gotten to know Jimmy. He's a great kid. We can't let him die.

"Call the Vincent lab and ask them to manufacture one hundred milliliters of the common cold adenovirus at a concentration of $5x10^7$ infectious units per milliliter. We'll infuse our Gene P inside the virus here in the lab."

Azi had mastered English as easily as he mastered molecular biology, but he was not conversant with all the idioms. He burst out, "The price of steaks is going up."

Alex called across the hall to his assistant, Hilary Stout. "Hilary, please schedule an appointment with Drs. Colson and Thompson in the next couple of days. We can meet in Marty's office. Also, please tell Mrs. Higgins, when she brings Jimmy in a week from Friday for his routine intravenous nutritional boost, that I would like to speak with her in my office." Stout was a registered nurse by education and training who chose a career in medical office administration. She chose well. So did Alex. Stout earned her undergraduate degree from the University of Virginia on a volleyball scholarship. She was almost half a foot taller than Alex and she dressed tall—high collar, high heels, and high spirits—yet grounded and reliable. She was also competitive and tough. Alex counted on Stout, for sound office administration, advice, and a hearty laugh. She never let him down.

Alex opened an envelope he had been handed just before he entered the meeting. A note from one of the technicians informed him that the BALC/c mouse with the common cold virus had died. He wadded it up and tossed it across the room into the wastebasket. Alex gave no indication of the disturbing content of the note. He looked at Azi and said with a wink, "It's time to make history."

CHAPTER EIGHTEEN

The following Tuesday Alex entered the executive suite at Rosenbaum Hospital at seven forty-five, in advance of his eight o'clock appointment. Alex noted that not all of Logan Howell's money was confined to the items in his lab and on the Rosenbaum need list. The waiting room had been redecorated in deep maroon and pastel blue.

Alex walked past the reception desk and looked to his right. Rosanne Ross, the CFO, was in her office behind a glass panel. Alex stuck his head in and said, "Hey Rosie, I've been wishing to speak with you. Betsy and I would like to plant one of those $500 trees for the side yard planting initiative." Rosanne walked over to the door and offered her hand. Alex shook it vigorously and added, "Yes, we want to dedicate this to our puppy, Mendel. It would please us to know that Mendel will always have his own place to relieve himself when he visits me at the hospital."

"Seriously?"

Alex had already left Rosanne's office and was proceeding across the waiting room for his meeting with Colson. He had hoped to have five or ten minutes in private with his friend Marty, but when he entered the office, Colson was already immersed in a conversation with Margo Thompson.

Colson beckoned Alex to sit down on the white plush sofa. He sank in. Colson looked at Thompson and then to Alex and said, "Your meeting, Alex."

Alex took the signal and began, "As you know, for the past few years we have been working diligently at the Institute on Aging on a number of initiatives, including research on progeria. I would like to personally thank you, Margo, for the collegial collaboration in which we have been engaged. Jimmy Higgins has undoubtedly benefited. On a number of occasions, I have separately assured both of you that our institute has devoted many hours to this formerly intractable devastation. I say formerly, because we have developed a protocol for the treatment and perhaps cure of progeria."

Colson asked, "Would we be first in the world to proffer a cure?"

"Yes, Marty. We have kept up on the literature, and the disease remains in the incurable category."

Colson was animated. He said, "That's incredible. God bless you, Alex, for saving those poor children. This will be a great boon to our Institute on Aging and to Rosenbaum. How can the hospital cooperate? We can ..."

Thompson raised her hand. "Wait a minute."

Colson turned to her. "Yes, Margo?"

She questioned Alex, "Would the therapy y'all developed be characterized as experimental?"

"Yes, thankfully, it is."

"Then we must follow established guidelines."

Alex responded, "C'mon Margo. Guidelines? There are no guidelines or medical standards for a disease that only a handful of people have. Someone said, 'Old age is a massacre.' When defending a massacre, there can be no rules. It's like asking David to fight Goliath according to the rules of the Marquess of Queensberry."

Colson's enthusiasm was dampened. He said to both of them, "Yes, I suppose we should adhere to established procedures. We need to present it to the Rosenbaum Scientific Review Committee for approval of your science." Colson referred to his calendar. "They meet on the third Thursday of the month, let's see, that would be in three weeks. They usually deliberate for a week. We could have your answer in about a month. There is an appeal process. That would take a lot longer. Perhaps as much as six months." In the end, you should receive approval. You might be denied, or the committee may just kick it to NMAP."

Thompson said, "NMAP? Oh, right, National Medical Advisory Panel. I've never been in a situation before where I had to seek their guidance."

"Yes, Margo, that's an organization many smaller hospitals like ours rely on for advice on medical ethics."

Dr. Colson went on, "After approval of the Scientific Review Committee, your proposal will automatically go before our hospital's Institutional Review Board for a patient safety opinion. They'll want to review the animal studies that prove the safety of your protocol. The Committee will tolerate a degree of risk. That usually takes about four weeks."

Alex scooted to the front of the couch and started to stand but thought better of it. "We did not have time for animal studies." Alex's tone was measured. Before he could continue, Thompson said, "I'm sure the FDA will insist we conduct a trial."

Alex stood. "That's ridiculous, Margo. The FDA would only be concerned if we intended widespread distribution. After we deal with the few hundred existing cases, we'll only administer this therapy a few times a decade."

Thompson shook her finger at Alex and threatened, "I will not be spoken to t-t-thataway Dr. Morton." Thompson's next words could barely be heard. "Metronome, tick, tick, tick."

Alex took a deep breath and lowered his voice. "I'm sorry, Margo. You are a solid and caring practitioner. I know we both want what is best for Jimmy."

Colson looked at Alex and said, "Perhaps you are too quick to pigeonhole the FDA. That agency's research extends a bit father than you think, including the protection of public health by assuring the safety, effectiveness, and security of our drugs and vaccines."

Colson pleaded, "We can't be in a hurry, Alex. We need to follow the rules. Perhaps we should collaborate on a paper and submit it to a scientific journal."

Alex shrugged and faced his colleagues with his hands on his hips, "I *am* in a hurry. Every month's delay is like a year to Jimmy. He could never grow old because he *is* old. Even the most durable of these kids die in their teens. They're just kids. Every time I read when one of them dies, it makes me furious. Who could blame us for trying to cure Jimmy as soon as possible? These boards and panels will be responsible for Jimmy's death. Is this what we have in mind for Jimmy? We took the Hippocratic Oath. Doing nothing when we know death is imminent equates to doing harm in my book."

Alex persisted, "People don't understand that research is a cumbersome and complex process of designing experiments, collecting data, and evaluating results. The development of an ordinary drug from time of concept to production often takes more than a decade. Scientific journals, those smug self-appointed keepers of the gate, can easily take a year to grind through the various steps of their procedure, including the clucking of anonymous outside experts, known as peer review. Marty, progeria is one of the rarest diseases in the world. There are probably fewer than 400 cases worldwide. The kids don't all live in one place and they can't travel without risk. A trial would be impossible anyway. By the time I could mount a clinical trial meeting FDA standards, my subjects—including Jimmy—would all be dead. It's like the guy on Ed Sullivan trying to juggle a dozen dinner plates. Every day in my lab, I used to say, another day has gone by and I have no solution for that boy. Well, now I do."

Alex raised his voice, "Jimmy Higgins is entering his 'death zone.' He is nine years old, almost ten. A great majority of these kids do not reach age thirteen. Jimmy is already under siege with heart disease, high blood pressure, and a myriad of ailments befitting someone who is in his 80s."

Thompson interjected, "Alex, he's my patient too, and I do not approve of this procedure until the efficacy is proved to the highest scientific standards."

Colson added, "I think we can successfully petition our Institutional Review Board for an expedited hearing on the basis of a single-patient compassionate use. I'll put Wexler on that project as soon as we receive the okay from the Scientific Review Committee. As to referring your proposal action to our Scientific Review Committee, we must follow that protocol. Alex, I'll let you know when you are on their agenda and I promise, you can personally present the argument."

Colson stood. Thompson followed. "Before we end this meeting, I want to let you know on behalf of Rosenbaum and me personally, how much we appreciate the brilliant work of the Institute on Aging. Please don't let our requirement to follow hospital protocols dampen your enthusiasm. Thank you both for coming in this morning, and I'll be back in touch."

Alex called a meeting that same afternoon with Azi, two techs, and Alex's assistant, Hilary Stout. He entered the room without a hello and began speaking. "One day soon we may be granted the opportunity to administer our therapy to Jimmy Higgins, and we have to be prepared. I thought about a list of topics for us to discuss today, and I'll need your input.

"First, we may use the team that meets with Jimmy once a month to administer his intravenous nutritional enrichment therapy. That way we can dispense with issues of whether Jimmy needs sedation, anesthetic, special needles, and equipment given his size and weight. Hilary, please identify that team by names so that when the time is right, we can talk to them.

"We will need to prepare our solution and package it in the same way that he receives his nutrition every month. Azi, please put that together and let's make sure that our delivery pack is virtually the same as the delivery pack used routinely by the nurses administering nutrition to Jimmy.

"Hilary, get a copy of the release that Mrs. Higgins signs every time she comes in. I would like to read it and perhaps revise it to apply to our therapy.

"Next, we need to determine whether we prescribe additional nutritional supplements of any kind. What about prescribing medicine for the symptoms he's likely to incur after coming down with the virus?"

The group was unanimous that no more supplements were needed. They agreed that the Higgins boy was currently on a vigorous routine. Hilary quipped, "Jimmy Higgins is taking more pills than Elvis Presley."

Encouraged by the group's laughter, Hilary added her thoughts.

"I have a fear that the anti-viral compound we would use to combat the effects of the virus may retard the effectiveness of the virus to deliver Gene P." The group nixed anti-viral therapy.

"Does anyone else wish to raise an issue?"

Azi addressed Alex, "Perhaps we should alert Dr. Thompson when the appointment is made."

Alex nodded. "By all means, Azi, by all means. We will definitely alert Dr. Thompson at the appropriate time."

CHAPTER NINETEEN

Deborah Higgins arrived with Jimmy in tow at 8:30 in the morning. They had been through this drill many times. Jimmy carried his backpack containing the paperback volume of *Call of the Wild*, some math homework, and an Etch A Sketch. Mother and son were shown into Room Six to Jimmy's joy, who said to his mother, "I love this room. Look over there." Jiminy Cricket was lecturing to Pinocchio on the wall mural.

The IV nurses bustled about the room. One asked, "Jimmy where do you want the IV pole, left or right this time?"

Jimmy held up his left hand. "Left please. I don't want my right arm to be sore before my guitar lesson."

Hilary was waiting for them. She assisted Mrs. Higgins in unloading Jimmy's backpack while one of the nurses applied ELA-Max, an anesthetic cream, to the crook of Jimmy's left elbow. Hilary said, "Jimmy, you have a beautiful smile."

"Thank you, Nurse Stout. Do you know Dr. Smith?"

"Lambert? Of course."

"He pulled some crooked teeth and made room for my smile. Aren't I good lookin'?"

"You bet."

Hilary turned to Mrs. Higgins. "When you get settled in, please come up to the sixth floor and meet with Dr. Morton for a few minutes."

Hilary left the room. In three quick paces she hit the elevator up button. She did not bother to knock at the door to Alex's private office. She found him pacing the floor and said, "Mrs. Higgins will be up in a few minutes."

"Thanks, Hilary. I need to go on a little errand, and if I'm not back, please ask her to wait." Alex left Hilary in his office and went into the laboratory. He placed a package from the refrigerator in his attaché case and climbed down three floors on the back stairway. He returned to his office by elevator fifteen minutes later.

Azi watched him take a plastic bag from his attaché case and toss it into the medical waste receptacle. He caught Alex by the arm and said, "You made a switch?"

"Yes, Azi, I played a little trick on those guys in order to save a life."

Azi smiled and said, "I believe the word is 'bamboozle.'"

The receptionist informed Alex that Mrs. Higgins was waiting in his office.

Alex sat down on the chair next to Mrs. Higgins. "Deborah, what's Jimmy up to?"

"Jimmy's grades are perfect. We have resisted attempts to treat him any differently from the rest of the kids in his class. His classmates are now nonchalant about the whole thing. He is learning to play the guitar. Jimmy will celebrate his tenth birthday soon. You will come to his birthday party?"

Alex responded, "I'll go anywhere for birthday cake and chocolate chip ice cream."

Alex reached over to his desk and handed Mrs. Higgins a consent form. Mrs. Higgins glanced at the form and said, "We already signed the standard release when we arrived today. It's the same form we sign every time we come in."

Mrs. Higgins took another quick look:

Rosenbaum Hospital Institute on Aging
CONSENT TO INTRAVENOUS TREATMENT

I, Deborah Higgins, mother of Jimmy Higgins, understand that Jimmy has been diagnosed with progeria and that Drs. Margo Thompson and Alex Morton, Jimmy's physicians, are members of the Rosenbaum medical staff and have recommended that my son receive the nutritional supplements and other medicine, including exploratory therapies for progeria.

I certify that Jimmy's physicians and I have discussed the proposed treatment to provide enrichment and to combat progeria. There is no guarantee that the therapy will produce the desired response or that it will not produce side effects that diminish my son's quality of life, including but not limited to the following: nausea, vomiting, diarrhea, constipation, appetite changes, taste changes, fatigue, facial flushing, swelling, muscle aches, fever, risk of infection, cough, shortness of breath, and joint inflammation.

I voluntarily give my consent on behalf of my son to receive the planned therapy. I may withdraw my consent at any time. My decision to stop receiving the planned therapy will not affect the willingness of my physicians to provide medical care now or in the future.

_____   _____
Date   Signed: Deborah Higgins

Alex replied, "This form is slightly different. It reflects the conversation we had last week about the experimental therapy we have developed. Thanks again, Deborah, for keeping this between ourselves." He pointed out a few lines that gave notice to Mrs. Higgins that the hospital may from time to time consider exploratory therapies in addition to supplemental nutrition. Mrs. Higgins signed and dated the form. She stood and turned to Alex.

"No parent should have to sign something like this, but God help me, I'll do anything to save Jimmy."

"So will I, Deborah. So will I."

Alex motioned to Mrs. Higgins. "I'll escort you back down to Jimmy."

She replied, "I know how to get around this hospital pretty well by now." They walked to the elevator. She pushed the down button and turned around and hugged Alex. "Thank you, Dr. Morton. We love you."

The next day at 1:00 a.m. Mrs. Higgins called Dr. Thompson. "Jimmy is spiking a fever of 105. He is congested and having trouble with his breathing."

Thompson said, "Call an ambulance. I'll meet you at Rosenbaum in 15 minutes."

Alex heard about Jimmy the next morning. Everyone was talking about Jimmy Higgins, the darling of Rosenbaum Hospital, who was fighting for his life on the third floor. Thompson maintained a bedside vigil most of the morning. That afternoon she called Doc Adams, who arrived 20 minutes later. Alex was in Jimmy's room when Doc arrived.

"Jimmy, how are you feeling?"

Jimmy managed a weak smile. He could barely speak and breathe at the same time, but he was game. He said, "Mom says I have a bad cold."

After 15 minutes with Jimmy, Doc turned to Margo and said, "You're doing all the right things trying to keep him cool with cold compresses, but he is still running 105. Based upon the

IV chart, you are trying to keep up with hydration. What else here?"

Margo replied, "He is on a course of Staphcillin."

"That won't work. Jimmy is coherent. If his temperature spike had been caused by a bacterial infection, he would be moribund. His blood pressure has cratered and his pulse is unsteady. Jimmy probably does not have a bacterial infection. Moms are often correct. He is presenting with an adenovirus—a bad cold. Margo, I suggest we run a virus scan on his blood sample STAT. We need to learn a little more here."

Alex broke in, "That won't be necessary. You nailed it, Milty. It's the adenovirus for the common cold."

Doc said, "Alex, you're not that good. How did you figure that out?"

"I gave it to him two days ago as a means to deliver a cure for his progeria."

Doc remained outwardly calm. He turned to Margo and said, "As we know, there is no specific treatment for adenovirus infections. We need to ride it out. Continue to check his oxygenation level. If he doesn't die in the next three days, we'll beat this thing."

Within the hour, Alex was called away from Jimmy's bedside to a confrontation with Drs. Colson and Thompson. Thompson said, "You switched the bags by Jimmy's bedside."

Colson put his hand on Alex's shoulder and said, "There is a distinction between risky behavior and flat-out stupidity. As of this moment I must suspend your privileges at Rosenbaum pending further investigation. If this little boy dies, we'll be sued not only by the Higgins family, but the Micah Davis gang and everybody else. The FDA will probably close our hospital. You might get jail time, and I'll be working as an orderly somewhere in Madagascar."

Thompson added, "And I'll kill you, Alex."

Two days later, Jimmy had diarrhea. His weight slipped to 28 pounds. His lungs began to fill with fluid and his blood pressure fell. His kidney function flagged. Jimmy lost consciousness that evening. He was moved to intensive care.

Dr. Thompson placed an anxious call to Doc. "Jimmy is dying! It is harder and harder for him to take a breath. I am going to put him on a respirator."

"Margo, that is a dark alley from which he is not likely to return. His body is attacking the virus and his immune system is overreacting. Instead, dose him with immunosuppression D and super-oxygenate him until his levels are back up to 97 percent. Run his blood through dialysis and ice him down to one hundred degrees. Hold your respirator as a last and desperate weapon."

That evening, Deborah Higgins called the family priest, Father Hendricks, who hurried to Jimmy's bedside. Father Hendricks had spent many hours with Jimmy and Mrs. Higgins over the past few years offering advice and consolation. He was a family friend. As soon as Father Hendricks entered the room, the attending doctors and nurses quietly slipped into the hall.

At Jimmy's bedside Father Hendricks chanted, "In the name of the Father, and the Son, and the Holy Spirit, as he made the sign of the cross. Mrs. Higgins also made the sign of the cross. Father Hendricks produced a gold container the size of a cap from a two-liter coke bottle. Inside the container was a cotton ball soaked in olive oil blessed by the church. He pressed his thumb on the cotton ball until it was covered with the blessed oil. On Jimmy's forehead he traced his thumb with the sign of the cross. He did the same on each of Jimmy's palms as he said, "Through this holy anointing may the Lord in his love and mercy help you with the grace of the Holy Spirit." Father Hendricks beckoned Mrs. Higgins close to the bed and together they said, "Hail Mary, full of grace, the Lord is with thee. Blessed are you among women, and blessed is the fruit of your womb, Jesus. Holy Mary, mother of God, pray for us sinners, now and at the hour of our death. Amen." Father Hendricks led Mrs. Higgins to two chairs at the end of the bed. He took her hand in both of his and said, "Deborah, Jimmy is in the lap of the Lord. If your son leaves this earth, he will be in the lap of the Lord for eternity. Please know that his travails will be at an end. When he arrives at the gates of heaven Jesus, our savior, will collect his soul."

Mrs. Higgins said, "Father Hendricks, Jimmy is in an unconscious state but I know your presence and our prayers will permeate his consciousness and provide encouragement in his fight for life on this earth."

Alex re-entered the room on tiptoe. He offered his hand to Father Hendricks in thanks. As Father Hendricks left the room, Alex signaled for the attending medical personnel to resume their duties.

Alex and Margo spent much of the next three nights with Mrs. Higgins. While Margo looked on Alex with disdain, his friend Marty didn't have the heart to boot him from the hospital. Doc visited twice daily. Gradually Jimmy's vital signs returned to normal and on the fifth day he sat up in bed. He turned to Doc with a smile and said, "Boy, you know what really sounds good to me? A chocolate milkshake."

Two months later, Hilary harvested a tissue sample with a buccal smear swab inside Jimmy's mouth and delivered it to Azi in the lab. There was no sign of progeria.

CHAPTER TWENTY

A few months later the Mortons and Adamses met for dinner. Sunday night was pizza night—usually at Betsy's favorite joint, Amore's. It was located at the end of a narrow brick lane in Zionsville, a sleepy town in Boone County, northwest of Indianapolis. It was a fifteen-minute drive from the Mortons' Carmel home—fifteen minutes and fifteen years. The Zionsville Town Board managed a policy of zero growth. Developers complained that construction permits were issued on the third full moon of the month. The Zionsville Historical Society opposed teardowns and supported strict adherence to the commercial restrictions enacted in the early '50s. The town was like a grand dame growing past middle age and wearing the same dress. Local folks liked it that way. So did visitors, including Alex and Betsy. Betsy grew up in Carmel, a once sleepy town governed by a different philosophy. Carmel boasted the title, "Fastest-growing city in America."

Andreas Amore was an authentic Italian-American whose accent was as thick as the cheese on his pepperoni pizza—the specialty of the house. One would have to go to New York to get a better slice.

Everyone in the Amore kitchen knew Alex and could hear him coming in his powder blue Corvette. Alex caught Andreas's eye from across the room. "Andy, I'll have the DaVinci tonight. Betsy will have the usual. Maybe a half order of that lasagna too. The Adamses are on their way. He had to stop for a house call."

Alex and Betsy had experience with Doc's Sunday evening house calls. They found the only available corner table and did not wait to eat dinner. Alex's pizza-eating technique is best described as "fold and stuff." Betsy's enjoyment at Amore's was only slightly less exuberant.

Halfway through dinner, the Adamses arrived and exchanged hugs. The Sunday noise level was just high enough to accord a private conversation. The men talked shop.

"Alex, how's Jimmy?"

"He's alive, thanks to you. At his last exam he was back up to 38 pounds. Last month he celebrated his tenth birthday. Betsy and I were invited to the party. The kid smiled all afternoon. He had lots of school friends sharing cake and ice cream. He's smart too. After the party I accepted his challenge to play children's Scrabble. He scored well—two six-letter words—until he ran out of energy—just crashed. Deborah said he has gained more energy every month. I think his disposition and the social inter-action have meant a lot to his survival. He has a loving mother. I have a special relationship with Deborah. She always trusted me. She took Jimmy to Disneyland, where he joined his pen pal, Jonesy, a progeric from Mason City, Iowa, and other stricken progeria boys and girls about his age. They all have gone through, or will undergo, the protocol we prescribed. Margo is now fully in charge of Jimmy's care. She is stressing a high-nutrition diet and has Eric Prystow dealing with his cardiovascular system in an attempt to restore and maintain his vascular integrity." Alex paused as Doc ordered the pepperoni pizza for himself and Janie.

Alex began again, "I'm on the agenda for the next meeting of the Progeria Research Foundation, where Azi and I will present our findings. Marty is facilitating a filing with all of the appro-priate authorities both inside and outside the hospital. Wexler is pursuing legal protection on behalf of Rosenbaum, which may include patent protection for Gene P, which we will probably turn over to the National Institutes of Health.

From here out, age progression will proceed at maybe even less than a normal pace because of the youthful Gene P. What I am worried about is what progeria has left in its wake. Think of the Higgins boy's body as a Kansas town that has been hit by a tornado. It is quiet—eerily peaceful, but so battered that a comprehensive cleanup may not be possible. I am also worried about Jimmy's mental condition. He is human. He needs to find love and meaning to his existence. I am struck by his courage and humbled by his spirit.

"We need to treat these progeria babies before outward signs appear. Even better, at birth—before the tornado hits. Since this disease affects only one in eight million, unless we find a unique marker in the blood or urine, the yield on tests would make the procedure cost-prohibitive. The only exception is the Walker baby. Through her network of progeria mothers, Deborah learned that Mrs. Walker was about to give birth to her second child. Because this disease is due to a gene disorder, there was a stronger probability that this new baby would have progeria. I flew to Omaha day before yesterday and tested this child within twenty-four hours of her leaving the womb. She tested positive. I know of no other sibling cases, so maybe progeria is a sporadic mutation after all. Hopefully, the therapy I recommended will render the disease powerless to wreak its havoc. We both know now it is not without risk."

Doc's pizza arrived but he didn't touch it. "Speaking of risk, Alex, you thumbed your nose at protocol and medical standards for new therapies. Janie and I are concerned for your reputation and even your license to practice medicine. It took a lot of lobbying to get your privileges back at Rosenbaum."

"You know, Milty, I may be a villain at Rosenbaum, but I am a hero in Omaha and everywhere else where mothers are caring for children with progeria."

Janie looked at Betsy and said, "Milt is right. Alex went off half-baked again."

Alex protested, "Again? I've never done that."

Betsy argued, "You always do that. In medical school didn't you jeopardize your whole career and our relationship by being a ski bum for three weeks?"

"*Ski instructor*, but okay, I was a touch impetuous. And what about you, Betsy? You weren't the most rational coed in the Pi Phi house. How many nights did you dance without your panties at the Timber Tavern?"

Betsy took another bite of her pizza. Then spread her arms apart palms up and tilted her head to the side. "When we met, you wouldn't let me go. I didn't know whether to get a restraining order or just give up and move in with you. You were intense. It wasn't the romance I always dreamed about."

"I won you, didn't I?"

"Yes, and I love you, Alex."

"Well, I am still intense. Milty, you mean more to me than anyone except for family. I want you to understand how I feel. Throughout this ordeal I was plagued by guilt and doubt. Nevertheless, I fought for that kid's life. I jeopardized my career in a battle to do my duty as a physician. And we won! Jimmy won! In the process we have established a framework for curing other formerly intractable single-defective-gene diseases, including Huntington's disease and sickle-cell anemia, but those opportunities are left for others to tackle. Sometimes I am a bit reckless, usually followed by periods of sincere regret. Thank you and Janie for your friendship and wise counsel.

"We have a new battle ahead of us. The work on progeria over the last few years provided me with a better understanding of cell death and what occurs in the body as we all grow older. I now have ideas and theories to pursue in order to tackle an even more pervasive condition, which affects us all. I'm talking about death from old age.

"Life extension has never been a national priority like the space program. Even today, aging is an area of biology that we know almost nothing about and sparks little interest from the scientific community. It's no wonder. For centuries, the search for the Fountain of Youth has been associated with snake oil salesmen. If society created a trillion-dollar, multidiscipline assault on aging and death, we could produce dramatic results.

We could answer the question of why we decay as we grow older and why our living cells deteriorate. We could possibly extend life not incrementally, but exponentially. Maybe we could even figure out how to turn back the biological clock."

Janie smiled at her friend Alex. "Nothing lives forever."

"You are incorrect, Janie. There is a jellyfish known as *T. dohrnii* that has the primordial power of rejuvenation. It is made up of cells that can reverse course to become juvenile cells and seems to be functionally immortal. You like to swim don't you, Janie? If I figure this out, I am going to turn you into an immortal jellyfish."

Alex turned to Doc. "Milty, maybe we could change our evolutionary destiny—pick the genetic lock. Our lives would be more exciting than ever—forever. Aging is the mother of all diseases. There is no goal more seductive than extending human life. I'm rededicating my life to the fundamental study and prevention of aging, the greatest achievement of all time.

"I am searching for the Methuselah Gene."

PART TWO
METHUSELAH GENE

CHAPTER TWENTY-ONE

"Welcome to our inaugural Conference on Aging. I am Dr. Martin Colson, president of Rosenbaum Children's Hospital, and it is my pleasure to convene this conference. I see a number of you are standing in the back. We are bringing in more chairs, but we do need to begin on time today. Thank you for coming. As you can see, we have an enthusiastic response and why not? Aging affects us all. Because of recent advances in this space, interest has intensified. Not even 100 years ago, the average life span was under fifty. Someone born today in the United States can expect to live past seventy. You have heard the saying, 'It's not the cards you're dealt—it's how you play.' Well, our institute seeks not only to help you play, but to reshuffle the deck to give you a better hand.

Rosenbaum Children's Hospital has been serving our community for more than seventy-five years. Our staff of dedicated pediatricians and other specialists join us from all over the country. Their research and leadership have been influential throughout the world. Only recently have we turned our attention to aging. You might find that an odd direction for a children's hospital. Let me explain. Our interest arose through the treatment of the childhood disease progeria, a devastating and terrifying disease and until recently one thought to be unsolvable. Let's pause for a moment so I can introduce you to Dr. Alex Morton, a member of our pediatric oncology staff. He will join us as a panel member this morning. His discoveries and that of his team have led to the cure of progeria, the childhood disease that caused extreme aging and premature death. That's right, no child will need to suffer from this dreaded disease again. Alex, please stand." As he got to his feet, Alex said to himself, "Betsy was right. I am glad I wore this gray suit rather than the scrubs I originally had on." Everyone accorded Alex a standing ovation. Rosanne stamped her feet. Others followed. The foot stomping took on a rhythm. The boisterous response permeated the hospital like the sound of a rocket launch. Colson finally asked, "Everyone, please be seated so we can begin our program." When the assemblage quieted, Alex leaned over and whispered to Colson, "From pariah to paragon in six months. Thanks, Marty. I do appreciate the flattery, but you know, I would rather be in my lab."

Colson began again, "Our institute continues groundbreaking research on a myriad of complex issues. Because of the work of Alex Morton and his team, we are recognized as an influential leader in bioresearch. It is our responsibility to convene conferences such as this, and we are pleased to accept that role. Joining Alex Morton on our panel this morning is our moderator, Tom Harton, science and health editor of *Indianapolis Business Journal*, one of the sponsors of this conference. He will introduce the rest of our panel."

Colson sat down as Harton rose to polite applause. "Thank you, Dr. Colson, *IBJ* is pleased to co-sponsor this event and it is an honor for me to facilitate this extraordinary panel. You have already been introduced to Alex Morton, so allow me to introduce the other three esteemed guests. Please hold your applause until I have finished with the introductions.

To my far right is George Romig. He is the director of the University of Colorado Institute of Ethics and Health Policy. To his left is Miriam Isaacs, the Daniels Professor of Philosophy at Princeton University and director of its program on Medicine, Technology, and Society. She was also the medical consultant for the film, *Lacy Was Nobody's Child,* a winner of the NAACP Image Award. And to my immediate left is Arthur Hill, president of Genemics, whose investors have anted $1 billion for research in geronomics.

Today's topic is living forever—how will our society survive? At this time, I'll ask Rosenbaum's own Alex Morton to make an opening statement."

Alex flipped on his mic and began. "Thank you for your heartfelt applause upon my earlier introduction. Spending time in a laboratory bent over a Spectron microscope is a solitary endeavor. Perhaps that is why I enjoy it so much. Medical breakthroughs, however, are almost always a team effort. Please let me introduce to you a remarkable scientist who worked side by side with me in the lab and whose creativity and judgment were instrumental in our success, our team leader, Dr. Azayiz Dansinghani." Azi stood and slightly bent to the assemblage. His gesture was met with warm applause.

Alex continued. "Through the ages our magnificent profession has been noted for sharing and cooperation. Old discoveries have provided the platform for new discoveries. Recently, our colleagues at the Cleveland Clinic have tweaked the viral vector we used to deliver the progeria therapy. They succeeded in removing the DNA from the virus and rendered it incapable of replacing itself. I am pleased to share with you that because of their work, not only will progeria patients be cured, they will no longer have to embark on a perilous journey to get there. I was informed that the Division of Cardiovascular Medicine at Vanderbilt University is mounting a clinical study using our protocol. I can also report that I received a note last week from colleagues at Cambridge, who are using our replacement technique to treat blindness caused by a defective gene.

"We are busy at our institute investigating what makes our bodies tick, but more specifically, what makes our bodies stop ticking. We are scientists, but we like to think of ourselves at the Institute on Aging as thoughtful, caring human beings. We understand that, regardless of what science makes possible for the individual desire, aging is a public issue with social consequences, and these must be addressed. That is why I am fully invested in our topic this morning and am looking forward to hearing from fellow panel members.

"Here are a few questions our panel may address: Most of us would like to live radically longer, but can society afford that? Do we have the capacity to make our ultra-long lives fulfilling and enjoyable? What role would religion play, if any? Would radically long lives exacerbate the world population crisis and lead to overpopulation scenarios of scarce resources? Will we as humans become a form of planet pollution? Would increasing the average age to 250 be seen as an enormous biological victory or will it signal the death knell of the human race? I don't know whether we'll have answers today, but we will have a good time with our dialogue. Tom, let's begin."

Tom Harton assumed control of the meeting. "Professor Isaacs, why don't you launch our dialogue? I'll expect others on the panel to challenge you and each other. We are hoping for a spirited exchange. But before we begin, Dr. Colson wanted me to remind you, as a courtesy to your fellow attendees, to try to get to your breakout sessions at 1:30 sharp. Also, I note that there are still a few seats available for our $1,000-per-plate dinner tonight. This will give you an opportunity to speak with our panelists on a one-on-one basis and to provide thanks to the Rosenbaum Institute on Aging. Professor Isaacs."

Professor Isaacs leaned forward and said, "Thank you, Mr. Harton. First, I would like to say mazel tov to Alex and his team." She held heavy rimmed eyeglasses in her right hand and gestured with her left as she made her first point. "If we're going to extend the life span of the human species, we have to do so in a way that maintains our good health. Even today, 80 percent of a person's lifetime healthcare expenditures are spent on chronic diseases and end-of-life costs. Also consider, this mass of burgeoning elderly will have too few young people to care for them and ..."

George Romig took Harton's cue and interrupted Isaacs in midsentence. "Aren't we already seeing the consequences of pushing our life spans: Alzheimer's disease, dementia, joint and hip problems, and loss of muscle mass? "I don't want a life long on years and short on quality. I don't want to spend the next fifty years in a nursing home. As John Wayne used to say, 'I want to die with my boots on.' Today the odds of living a long life that's also a healthy life are slim. Does an aging society have to be a decrepit one? If so, then I recommend we let death have its day."

Before Professor Isaacs could begin again, Arthur Hill entered the fray. His attire voiced his departure from the corporate titans of the day, a snug-fitting black turtleneck rather than the three-piece suit expected of corporate officers. He wanted his associates to admire his sculpted sixty-three-year-old physique. They did. His voice was deep and slightly hoarse. He nodded his head at Harton. "Yes, our cost of medical care has gone up and we do spend a lot of money on the elderly, but the cost is incurred because there is an ever-growing list of useful things that doctors can now do to prolong our lives, and these are expensive. Consider cardiac pacemakers, artificial knees, shoulders and hips, and brain implants to help control tremors brought on by Parkinson's disease. If we're going to extend our years on this planet, then we need to understand and build in these increased costs along the way. Again, these costs are not for the decrepit aging population referred to by Miriam and George, these costs are for the active population who need to spend money for sophisticated tests, organ replacement, and an array of specialists who have the tools to extend our factory warranties—keep our bodies healthy while we double our life span. You want a good business tip? Once we discover how to double our life spans, go out and buy stock in homebuilders."

Harton tried to find consensus. "Let's agree that no one wants to grow old like the struldbruggs of "Gulliver's Travels," living forever but subject to aging and disease. No matter how long we're going to live, we all want to be vigorous and not a burden on our society until that day comes. Better to be like mole rats, who don't just live a long time, but are able to maintain excellent health until extreme old age. If we can do that, everybody wins."

Arthur Hill interjected, "Not so fast, Tom. Everybody wins? What about all those family members waiting for you to die so they can inherit your fortune?"

Harton paid no attention as he continued. "It's agreed. Society needs to focus on 'health span,' the number of years we spend free from disease, disability, and impairment. Remember Eos, the Greek goddess who fell in love with the mortal Tithonus? She asked Zeus to give her lover the same eternal life she enjoyed, but she failed to ask for eternal health for him, too. Tithonus aged, sickened, and withered. He wished for death but he could never die.

"Let's move past the concept of 'health span' and turn our attention to what our society might look like if the average life span is more than twice what it is today, let's say, 200 years."

Romig spoke directly into his mic, "I'll try to field that inquiry. At my age, almost 80, it would be nice to be able to look forward to another hundred years. Our CU program of ethics and health policy has examined that issue. Society will need to make some adjustments. A midsixties retirement age is not compatible with radical longevity and will have to be extended. You would expect the elderly to make contributions for at least another fifty years in the workplace and elsewhere at least part-time, and remain active for most of their lives."

Hill broke in, "You're right, George, because it doesn't take a mathematical genius to determine the current pension system would go broke."

Alex added, "Social Security is already on life support. Our political leaders just don't know it yet. Social Security and our health system would need to be realigned to the needs of our radically aging population. But there is a bright side to this. Think of our famous entertainers, scientists and leaders who will have many more years to enrich our lives in exchange for the burden their long lives may place on our youth. I, for one, could use another decade of Einstein's theories. Or how about another three dozen songs from Cole Porter, or more statesmanship from Thomas Jefferson, more short stories from Kurt Vonnegut. And we could all use additional moral guidance and passion from Martin Luther King.

Isaacs broke in, "Or you, Alex. You defeated a once intractable disease. I sure would like to see what you could do in the next 75 years."

"Thank you, Miriam."

"But Alex, Martin Luther King is not a good example. He was murdered.

Dealing with bigotry-induced malfeasance is beyond the scope of today's conference."

Harton let the dialogue run for twenty more minutes until he intervened once more. "Let's talk about a couple more issues. In our new society, if the well-aged stay in place, wouldn't that thwart the advancement of our youth and close out better opportunities? And what can society do with all those super-elderly, all those great-great-great-great-grandparents who view life extension as just more years of retirement? And finally, what if the life-extension opportunities are so expensive that society as a whole cannot afford them and they are only available to the super-rich? And another question, is it selfish to spend research money for rich people to live longer versus spending money on, say, malaria, to save millions of lives? How will we decide?"

Colson couldn't help himself. "Good point, Tom. Is it egocentric to enable the rich to grow richer and younger while the poor grow poorer and older? Rosenbaum has never turned away a needy patient. Even today the life expectancy difference between men at the top 10 percent of the wealth ladder and the lowest 10 percent is more than a dozen years. If we don't reduce disparities between rich and poor, America will regret it for many reasons, including the disintegration of our society to class warfare, another topic beyond the scope of today's conference."

Romig said, "The idea that resources might be better spent trying to delay aging rather than to cure diseases flies in the face of most disease-related philosophy. I would resist an effort to shift funds away from cancer and diabetes, where there are clear drug-therapy targets."

Alex was quick to respond. "You are missing an important point here, George. Aging is the biggest factor in virtually everything that kills us today. Scientists with sufficient resources to work on the complex issues of aging will, in fact, contribute to the cure of many of today's major scourges, including heart disease and cancer. Just suppose, George, that our aging studies discover a compound that would boost HDL levels in people who are at a higher-than-normal risk of having a heart attack. We can draw an analogy to the car racing industry that gave us sideview mirrors and NASA, which came up with memory foam."

Isaacs responded, "I'm not sure I have all the answers to your questions, probably none of us do, but deciding who gets to live longer smacks of Hitlerism. In the '40s, the Nazis decided to exterminate most of those who weren't of Arian derivation. Your question borrows that philosophy if you are saying some authority should be able to determine not who should die, but who should live or live longer than others. It's pretty much the same thing. Both results are unacceptable to a just society." She put her glasses back on, shook her luxuriant gray hair and pointed her finger at Hill and said, "You financial guys are going to have to figure that one out. Maybe capitalism doesn't hold up in our new society."

Hill stared back at Isaacs and said, "Capitalism is ugly, it's messy, it's inefficient, and objectionable in many ways, but it's the best system we've got. It's better than anything else that's ever been tried in the history of our world."

"Hang on there," Alex cut in. "Let's make it clear that American capitalism has a healthy dose of socialism mixed in, just in case you folks forgot about Medicare and Medicaid."

"Okay, okay," Hill gently patted the table, showing he wasn't seeking a fight on the topic. I'm just saying we can cheat death without cheating the poor. We'll be ready. When we sit around the Genemics corporate table and think about aging, we think about opportunities in business. For example, bionics: the augmentation or replacement of biological functions with machines and what will society pay for that? What is the role of bioengineering in the manufacture of body parts, hearts and arteries, and even noses?"

Romig still had the look of the all-American lineman he had been almost 60 years before. He had a barrel chest and evidence of his once youthful muscle tone; one would have thought he had discovered his own program of healthy aging. He said, "We talk a lot about what the planet would look like under radically long lifetime scenarios, particularly if they lead to overpopulation. Do we need to start contracepting and otherwise curbing births?"

Isaacs cut in, smiling, "Would you capitalists consider castration?"

Romig continued, "What is the role of sex in our new society? Today we think of sex in the same vein as conception. Would we separate those two notions? Would sex be only for pleasure? What about the institution of marriage? With an average life expectancy of two hundred years, we might see age differences of as much as 100 years between spouses, or would we invent other forms of relationships to supplement marriage? That vow 'until death do us part' will be as old-fashioned as shoes and rice."

Hill warmed to this question, "I have some pals who marry often. Given enough time, they would break Elizabeth Taylor's record. I personally would not bet on marriage to stand the test of time. I've tried it twice and neither lasted ten years." A few in the audience chuckled.

Isaacs turned to Hill and said, "I'll tell you a societal burden, dealing with our mental state. As we grow older, will we all become more set in our ways and resistant to change? Would we become depressed when time loses its significance and meaning, or maybe just plain bored? Do we have to grow old so sadly?"

Alex replied, "I read a study that suggested, on average, better-educated people suffer less mental deterioration in old age. Perhaps society should prescribe continuing education. A fair question to ask is 'How long do you want to live?' Personally, I'm one of those who would love to live another couple of hundred years. How about living longer and having more fun? Who wouldn't want to live long enough to shoot their age in a game of golf? I think there is so much more we can do for and with our friends, our family, and our society if we are granted that gift. I would look forward to continuing to make contributions during that entire life span. I would view 200 more healthy years as a blessing."

Isaacs said, "I agree with you, Alex. We should use the time to enjoy family and friends. That would certainly improve our mental state. That is, if society treats its aging population with more care and respect than it does today. Ageism is just as pervasive as sexism and racism. It takes many forms, including prejudicial attitudes and discriminatory practices, to name two."

Romig said, "In Colorado we are a bunch of environmentalists, I know, but Alex and Art, let me tell you that all of your work on aging and your rosy outlook could very well come to naught. You see, our institute has modeled the effects of "unnatural" death from bacteria, viruses, and accidents. We included in our model the effects of exploding global population, nuclear wars, and environmental disasters. Arthur, how much of that billion dollars in your wallet are you spending on inadvertent climate modification and arms control? At the CU Institute most of us believe that, unless those problems are solved, the human race on our planet Earth won't last another 300 years."

Harton stood up, spread his arms as if to embrace his colleagues and said, "On that cheery note I'm sorry to say our time is up. Please offer your thanks to our panel. You have time to eat lunch and still get to your breakout sessions. Be punctual. Remember, if you enjoyed the dialogue today, you have an opportunity to stay and join us for dinner tonight."

The audience gave a strong applause of appreciation while the panel members shook hands and engaged in informal conversations with each other and a few members of the audience.

Alex paused in front of Romig as they were leaving in opposite directions and said, "You need to imagine that a 200-year-old version of you and other environmentalists will have that much more time to figure out solutions to many of the earth's problems. We might treat our planet with greater care if we knew we would be around to suffer the effects of our disregard for its welfare." Romig shrugged and kept walking.

Colson did his best to stifle a yawn. He smiled. It wasn't even 7:30 that morning while tying his red power tie that his wife, Teddi, tackled him in the closet. He thought, "What's a guy to do? She was completely naked. She can be quite persuasive in an outfit like that."

CHAPTER TWENTY-TWO

At 3:30 on Tuesday afternoon, Yosso answered the ring on his office phone. "Ward, it's Teddi Colson. I would like to come in for a consultation."

"Of course, Teddi, but aren't you pleased with the doctor I referred to you, Dr. Patterson in our office?"

"She's fine. I'm very pleased. But I need some personal advice from someone with a little bit more seasoning. How soon can I come in?"

Yosso glanced at his schedule and said, "Teddi, we are full this week, but I suppose if you want to come in at the end of the day on Thursday, we can make that work."

"Okay, fine, Ward, I'll be there."

At 5:30 on Thursday afternoon, Yosso escorted Teddi Colson into his private office. They sat across from each other, she on the couch and he on the side chair. Teddi leaned back and blurted in one quick sentence, "Marty and I have not had sex for six months and I don't know, I just don't know. I do know it's not his fault. It's mine. There is something going on and I just don't want to have sex anymore."

Yosso leaned forward in his chair and held Teddi's hand. "Teddi, there is no reason to panic about this. First of all, you are not unique. Sexual dysfunction has been estimated to affect 40 percent of women in the general population. Also, Teddi, female sexual arousal disorders correlate significantly with increasing age. There are a number of reasons this could be happening, both physical and mental.

Let's go over a few questions."

"Okay, Ward." She looked into his eyes and squeezed his hand.

"Do you experience recurrent or persistent genital pain during sexual intercourse?"

"No."

"There is nothing in your chart about diabetes. Have you recently been diagnosed with diabetes?"

"No, doctor."

"Have you experienced lubrication failure?"

"No, doctor."

"Have you recently experienced depression or acute anxiety?"

"No, doctor."

"Have you recently experienced a general deterioration in your relationship with Marty?"

"We get along fine."

"Have you had any recent orthopedic surgeries?"

"None."

"I'm not sure I can advise you on the mental side, but would you like me to perform a pelvic examination? That would reveal any physical abnormalities including any lesions or other reasons for this situation. We can also measure your response to pressure and touch.

"Okay, let's at least do that."

They arose from their seats and Yosso escorted Teddi to an examining room. "Teddi, remove your clothes and hang them up in the closet. Put on one of these gowns, then have a seat on the examination table and I'll be in shortly." As he walked out, he turned back and said, "The examining room nurses have gone for the day. Would that be okay?"

Teddi replied, "Well I was your patient through two pregnancies, so I suppose that will be fine."

Five minutes later Yosso entered the examining room. He had changed his clothing and was now clad in surgical scrubs. Teddi lay back, bent her knees and allowed Yosso to place her feet in the stirrups and separate her gown. She relaxed as Yosso put on his gloves, applied a lubricant to the speculum and began the examination. He said, "I see nothing out of order here. You have healthy tissue, pink and shiny. Perhaps you've lost some sensitivity. I'll check that next." He took a silver probe from his tray and gently tapped it between her legs.

"Doctor, that's cold. Don't you have anything warmer?"

"I'm sorry. He put the probe on the tray and traced his finger lightly up and down. Teddi, do you feel that?"

"Yes, doctor."

Yosso peeled off his gloves.

"How about here?"

"Yes, doctor."

Yosso applied a little more pressure and moved a little quicker. "And here?"

"Yes, doctor."

He continued. First with one finger and then with two and then more rapidly in a clockwise rhythm.

"Yes, doctor. Yes, doctor." Teddi began to breathe heavily. "Yes, doctor. Yes, yes, YES!" She shuddered out a lot of low yeses. Yosso removed his hand and freed Teddi from the stirrups. She sat up and smiled at Yosso. She said, "You shouldn't have done that."

Yosso grinned, "How was the experience?"

She said, "Splendid. I don't know whether to sue you or thank you."

He replied, "Look at it this way. We found out that your problem with Marty is not within your own body. And you did say it was a splendid experience. I wouldn't exactly describe my experience as splendid."

Teddi said, "I guess you're right." She put her legs over the side of the table and stood up to let her gown drop to the floor. She dropped to her knees as she yanked down Yosso's scrubs. She reached behind him and grabbed both cheeks. As she pulled him toward her, she opened her mouth.

CHAPTER TWENTY-THREE

Alex wiped from the corners of his mouth the crumbs of a turkey sandwich Betsy had sent with him that day. He glanced at his watch, 6:58, as he opened the door to convene the meeting he had called for 7:00 sharp. Each attendee had accepted a role in the Institute on Aging's preliminary study titled, *Investigation of the Effect of Normal First Chromosome-Gene P on Lamin A.*

Colson had chosen not to participate, citing a conflict of interest with his role as CEO, and formally appointed Dr. Jessup as a Rosenbaum Hospital liaison to the study. Alex designated the Jester as a co-investigator. He accepted the appointment with enthusiasm. Alex also invited Margo Thompson to join the committee. She declined without further comment. Dr. Joseph Bennett, senior researcher at MD Anderson, agreed to join the committee by telephone. Bob Block was invited to attend the organizational meeting to be honored and thanked for underwriting the cost of the study with a $300,000 grant. Alex's assistant, Hilary, was designated project coordinator and took notes of the meeting. Azi's title was co-lead investigator with Alex.

The Jester sat down next to Bob Block, reached in his pocket and offered Bob gummy bears. Block smiled and picked a green one and a red one and ate them both at the same time.

Alex welcomed all. "Most of you know each other, however, let me offer a short introduction of our treasured sponsor, Bob Block. Bob and his company are the largest owners of apartment dwellings in the Midwest and one of the largest in the entire country. Chances are, our doctors at Rosenbaum lived in Block apartments when they were interns and residents. Betsy and I lived in Block Manor for a short time until we bought our home. Bob has always been a friend and enthusiastic supporter of Rosenbaum Hospital, and we were fortunate to be able to call upon him once again.

"With us by telephone today is an esteemed colleague, my mentor at MD Anderson, Dr. Joseph Bennett. I owe a lot to this man for his careful guidance. He counseled me to accept the position here at Rosenbaum, although I will say Betsy had a lot to do with it.

"Again, welcome to our organizational meeting. We have employed ten temporary lab techs to harvest our samples, and we have arranged with Dean McKinney at Butler University School of Business to use his graduate students as data coordinators and statisticians. Marty has asked David Wexler to prepare a donor release form in addition to our standard hospital health evaluation questionnaire.

"We'll recruit 10,000 tissue and blood samples for this preliminary study. From our grant funds, due to the largess of Bob Block, we will offer $10 per volunteer. The study will be divided into five cohorts, arranged by age of 2,000 persons each: children to age 11, youth to age 25, mature adults to age 50, seniors to age 70, and elderly with no upper limit. I am also pleased to announce that Bob will encourage his employees to participate. The Happy Hour Nursing Home will provide access to their residents and we'll use their help to solicit other nursing homes in central Indiana.

"We will endeavor to recruit an equal number of males and females, but that breakdown need not be exact. We also recognize that this preliminary study will be subject to geographical bias. When we progress to a larger study, say 1 million tissue samples, we will adhere to more rigid controls to demographics, geography, and other aspects. We will, however, reject all those suffering from any of the ailments listed on the form unless the volunteer is in the aged cohort and is in remission. Vincent Laboratories will analyze our tissue and blood samples, except the first few, which will be processed in our lab. We expect to fill our census in ninety days and complete the study six months thereafter."

Alex asked Hilary to distribute the preliminary budget.

INVESTIGATION OF THE EFFECT OF NORMAL FIRST CHROMOSOME-GENE P ON LAMIN A

PRELIMINARY BUDGET

Rosenbaum Institute on Aging	$25,000.00
Vincent Laboratories	$80,000.00
10,000 incentive payments at $10 each	$100,000.00
Ten temporary lab techs at $3,000 each	$30,000.00
Two co-investigator stipends of $10,000 each	$20,000.00
Project coordinator	$10,000.00
Contribution to Butler University for data coordination	$10,000.00
Contingency	$25,000.00
TOTAL	$300,000.00

Our investigation will measure and compare the form and bonding ability of lamin A, the replication speed of the cell, the integrity of the nuclear membrane, and the number of senescent and dead cells in the sample. For the benefit of those who may not know, senescent cells are cells that linger in the body even after they have lost the ability to divide.

We will endeavor to reconvene our committee once a month. Meanwhile, work through Hilary, our project coordinator. Are there any questions?"

Block spoke slowly. He was accustomed to rapt attention. He took his time. "I have no questions, but would like to say how thrilled we are to support this initiative. Rosenbaum has been a godsend for our family ever since Marty Colson and Doc Adams took such good care of my darling granddaughter, Marietta. I remember when I was just back from the war, I met old Ike Rosenbaum. He would have been proud of what's going on here. I too am proud and pleased to be associated with Rosenbaum, a beloved institution in Indianapolis."

"I have a question." The Jester swallowed his candy and inquired, "What exactly are my duties as co-investigator?"

Azi replied for Alex, "Dr. Jessup, we will work together to guide the study, including troubleshooting in the event that recruitment, processing, and analysis does not proceed as planned. You will be tasked to share our progress with Marty and the hospital board at Marty's request. Finally, we are looking forward to harnessing your considerable analytical skills to evaluate what we have and to craft a plan for further studies."

The Jester popped in a malted milk ball, smiled, and nodded his approval.

After the meeting adjourned, Azi stayed back for a conversation with Alex. Alex said, "Azi, we know that our Gene P has an effect on premature aging of progeria patients and on reproduction of normal cells. Suppose this study informs us that Gene P gets a little tired after a while and gradually fails to provide for lamin A to work at its earlier pace and efficiency. Perhaps that is what causes the slower death of the cell that leads to normal aging. Armed with that knowledge, suppose we could then replace the Gene P from time to time, say every few years, with a brand-new Gene P. Could we, by doing that, retard aging, perhaps by fifty years or more?"

The next morning Alex invited Hilary into his office and shut the door. "Hilary, we are going to do a little remodeling around here. Please locate the blueprints for our offices. I am particularly concerned with the print of the radioactive room. In the meantime, ask maintenance to move the cryogenic tank that we are not utilizing in there and have it filled halfway with liquid nitrogen. Oh, and requisition two more fluorescent microscopes, please. I'll let you know what else we will need. The combination to the radioactive room is 090438 but don't write it down. Forward it to Marty. He'll need it in case something should happen to both of us. It's Betsy's birthdate.

Hilary noticed a new hanging next to the Monet. "Looks like you already began the remodeling."

"Hilary, that Monet is not mine. It belongs to Betsy, and the framed letter you see means more to me than any work of art." Hilary stepped closer to the wall. She saw a letter from Jimmy Higgins on lined elementary school notepaper. She moved her lips as she read the letter:

Dear Docter Moorton,

Thank you for saving my life. My mother told me you are a sant.

I am shur she is right.

Love,

Jimmy

******

By the time Alex and Azi had completed most of their analysis on the first 100 samples, they could accurately predict in which cohort the sample fit. Particularly telling was the degree of integrity of the nuclear membrane, the precursor to cell breakdown. Larger senescent cell counts added further confirmation to their predictions.

A week later Hilary met Alex in the hall and said, "I need to discuss something about our project with you and today wouldn't be too soon." Her somber demeanor sent an undeniable message.

Hilary usually provided the rosy spirit of camaraderie that percolated throughout the institute. Always smiling, her six-foot frame was usually clad in a skirt and starched shirt, with the collar popped in either bright red or Tiffany blue. Alex ushered her into his office. As soon as they sat down Hilary said, "We've got problems with our volunteer census. One, the techs at Vincent Labs found traces of recreational drugs and on a few occasions evidence of heroin and cocaine. They asked if that is acceptable or do we feel it will unduly skew our cell analysis?"

Alex drew a deep breath and shook his head. "I'm sorry I didn't think of this in advance, Hilary, but yes, we need to eliminate those samples. Drug use has a known dilatory effect on healthy cells. Please eliminate those samples. What else?"

Hilary smiled at Alex and said, "I thought of this myself. Many of our elderly and aged population have checked positive for cancer on their questionnaire."

Alex said, "I know, I know, Hilary. But we decided to accept them as long as they were in remission."

Hilary put up her hands to stop Alex's reply. "I agree, but have we ever determined whether those patients received radiation? And doesn't radiation have an adverse effect on cells, and wouldn't that also skew our results?"

Alex stood up and began to pace the floor. "Wow! You are correct, Hilary. We need to go back to those volunteers and ask whether they have received radiation therapy. If they did, we will have to eliminate them from our study. Good thinking, Hilary."

At the next regular monthly meeting of the committee, Hilary stood to report her findings. In her three-inch heels, she was a dominating presence. "Because we've had to eliminate a number of volunteers, we've found ourselves approximately 125 specimens short, spread over the older three cohorts: adult, elderly, and aged. That is not devastating, but we are striving for something closer to a 100 percent sample acceptance."

The Jester asked, "How did that happen?"

Hilary replied, "We eliminated many samples on the basis of drug use and some on the basis of prior radiation therapy. It is interesting to note that many of the volunteers we eliminated because of drug use provided no address on their forms. I don't mean to disparage the homeless, but I did do a little research and found, according to the Weller Mission Homeless Shelter, that drug use, at least marijuana, is prevalent among their clientele. We won't have lost any time if we can refill those cohorts in the next week or so. Hilary is going to call Alexis Wood at Eli Lilly and the folks at the Aron Nursing Home to fill the gaps. If any of you have other ideas, let me know."

Dr. Bennett's voice blared from the speakerphone in the middle of the table. "Ms. Stout, we would be happy to recruit volunteers from our staff and to take the interviews and harvest the samples to help you complete your census. At our research center we do this kind of thing all the time. Please let me know if you could use our help."

Alex met Hilary in the hall on his way to the elevator. She was sitting on a bench exchanging her heels for running shoes. He said, "Hilary, thanks again for your detective work and brilliant support over the last few weeks. You are an important member of our team."

She stood and clasped Alex's hand. "Alex, we are engaged in groundbreaking, maybe even perilous research. I am honored to be a loyal member of your team and will continue to be wherever that research may take us."

CHAPTER TWENTY-FOUR

The results were in. It was only Thursday afternoon, but the news was too exciting to wait another day. Alex and Azi sat across from one another in Alex's office. They went straight to the conclusion section, then reviewed the full report from Vincent Laboratories. Those outside of Alex's office could hear the occasional "huzzahs" from Azi. Alex enthused, "This data confirms our hypothesis. Gene P does not hold up well in the older cohorts, and its apparent influence on most data points, including the integrity of the nuclear membrane, leads to the preliminary conclusion that a refreshed Gene P will prevent or retard cell death in healthy normal samples, no matter which cohort. That would be one key to radical life extension."

Azi said, "Okay Alex, let's test that hypothesis in our flasks. Let's measure the influence of a fresh Gene P on cell death. Hopefully, we will see Gene P work its magic when we infuse a refreshed version. In that case, all the cells will look like cohort one and two."

Two weeks later, as Alex and Azi pored over the new data, they realized that even with the new Gene P, cell death was occurring only slightly slower. They looked at each other.

"What are we missing, Azi?"

"Well, the only thing that Gene P has no influence on is the number of senescent cells in the tissues. They just linger there after they have lost the ability to divide. One could conclude that cells are dying because neighboring senescent cells are interfering with normal cell life and replication. Based upon the relatively low senescent cell count in cohorts one and two, our younger demographics, it looks like the genes associated with senescence are dormant until the post-productive period. Is it the garbage in the tissue that is causing our cells to die in spite of a refreshed Gene P? Senescence is likely due to the action of several genes. Identification and modification of those genes within a reasonable time is beyond our capabilities. We cannot halt the cell senescence, but what if we remove the senescent cells, would we show better results?"

The scientists set up their next experiment with tissues from cohorts three, four, and five, from which they purged the senescent cells. They replaced Gene P with Gene P from their cache of foreskin. Over the next few weeks, they watched—and waited. The cells replicated in a normal manner and the tissues remained youthful and vigorous. Alex was ecstatic.

Azi interrupted Alex's celebration. "I have a few theories and concerns. Cellular immortality has a bad name in medicine. It's called cancer. Two, perhaps, no matter how often we refresh Gene P, cellular senescence may occur when the cells extinguish their telomeres. Three, senescent cells may appear to be dormant, but they may continue to perform vital functions. We cannot be sure what the side effects will be. Their removal could be fatal."

Alex replied, "Azi, don't you have anything positive to add to this dialogue?"

"No."

Alex was not as interested in Azi's theories as he was in confirming his conclusion. He said, "Azi, what governs life span is unrepaired damage—as we have shown in our studies of Gene P. The corollary to this theory is that removal of damaged and defective material in our cells is integrally important to the repair process." Alex hesitated for a moment and then added, "These senescent cells can't replicate. They are just sitting ducks for our therapy. They should be easy targets. All we need to do is to find a substance that will selectively destroy senescent cells. Let's find the garbage man."

"How do we do that?"

"Azi, I have no idea. Perhaps we're looking at this the wrong way. We know that each aging cohort contains more senescent cells than the younger cohorts. It's been proven that our immune system becomes less efficient as we grow older. Is there a correlation here? Could it be the immune system is supposed to sweep away senescent cells, to clean up the garbage? Instead of finding substances to remove senescent cells, why don't we assist the mechanism that's doing it already? Let's super-boost the immune system in cohorts three, four, and five and let those garbagemen do their jobs. Do you still have that tissue sample we took from Jimmy Higgins to prove that we had defeated progeria?"

Azi nodded his assent.

"Okay, do you recall the reaction that he had the days before when he almost died?"

Again, Azi nodded his head. "It was a cytokine storm, an out-of-control immune system caused by proteins, cytokines to be exact. Cytokines when not out of control are an integral part of the body's immune response. Doc knew it. If he hadn't insisted on dialysis to remove the cytokines from Jimmy's kidneys and blood system, Jimmy would have died."

Alex added, "That and the dose of immunosuppression D. Azi, count the senescent cells in that Higgins sample. I bet you won't find many."

Alex's hunch was correct.

"Azi, let's source the substances that we know or suspect will hyper-energize the immune system like a turbo-charged Corvette." Alex, mused, "I am sure there is a gene that directs the secretion of these enzymes, but we don't have time for another gene search."

The search lasted through the winter, a winter of the Americanization of Saima and a sisterhood with Betsy. The Dansinghanis learned to ski. Under the less than watchful eye of Alex, who shouted to Azi at the top of a black diamond slope, "Every man for himself," Azi flipped over a mogul and broke his right arm. Alex and Azi spent the next two days together in front of the ski lodge fireplace discussing their childhood experiences.

******

One spring morning Alex found Azi chuckling at his desk. He could not hide his smirk. "Alex, I was about to come into your office. Our team has found a substance that will hyper-energize the immune system and will remove the garbage. It's a compound in human semen called spermidine."

"Where did you get it?"

"A company in Delaware gave us a limited supply. It's a little much to ask volunteers—male volunteers—to contribute to our cause. Marty will not appreciate a Rosenbaum masturbation party." Azi's smirk developed into full-throated laughter.

Alex grinned. "We've done it then. We only need a small sample anyway and we can produce our own."

"Not me, Alex. I have a broken arm."

"Just make sure Hilary doesn't walk in on you."

In the midst of hearty laughter, Alex exulted, "Jabberjest!"

Azi corrected, "It's Zabardast!"

The animal tests were conclusive. The elderly mice given the cocktail of refreshed Gene P and spermidine fairly pranced about their cages. They did not develop cataracts and their muscles did not waste away with age. They lived twice as long, while the mice receiving refreshed Gene P without the full cocktail exhibited a lost energy level and lived a scant amount of time past their expected life spans. Autopsies on the fully dosed mice showed no sign of senescent cells.

Azi said, "We've done it."

Alex replied with a perfect, "Zabardast!"

CHAPTER TWENTY-FIVE

Betsy helped with the platters of potato salad and slaw. "Medium rare is fine for Alex and me, Janie. Put enough mustard on it and Alex will eat anything that doesn't move. We both love hamburgers."

"Saima?"

"We tend to the more medium."

Betsy poured the lemonade. She looked up and said, "Shall I go down to the pond and get the boys?"

Janie said, "I told Doc to stay only a few minutes. Azi wanted to see the Milton Adams bridge. Doc calls it the 'Block Bridge'."

Janie was right, by the time the women placed the food on the porch picnic table, the men had hiked up the path.

Doc welcomed their guests. "It is our pleasure to entertain our dear friends Betsy and Alex and join them in honoring Saima and Azi, who will leave us soon for a position at the UC-Berkley medical center to continue his work in exploratory medicine. Congratulations on finishing your fellowship at the IU medical school and for the quality years you have given us thereafter—and for enriching our lives while you were here. I will especially miss Faraz, one of the perfect children in my practice. Let's raise our lemonades in a toast to the Dansinghani family and their rich future. May it be filled with happiness."

Janie refilled the glasses and Alex toasted his tribute ending in "Azi, you are a brother to me."

Azi replied, "Saima and I came to Indiana with no family. You are our family."

The beautiful October day was turning windy. By the time dinner was finished, a chill was in the air. Janie went inside and returned wearing a sweater. She had a sweater in each hand. Betsy chose the red one.

After Saima and Alex had eaten their second hamburgers, Janie stood up and said, "Alex, come into the kitchen and I'll help you wipe all that mustard off your shirt." Betsy followed Alex and Janie. "We'll have dessert in the family room. Everyone please take a plate on the way in, and I'll serve homemade apple pie à la mode picked from our orchard just this morning." Janie took the pie from the windowsill and placed it on the wooden kitchen counter that doubled as a cutting board. She chose a knife from the wall among eight knives of various sizes hanging in a row.

Betsy looked up to see a number of pots and pans that dangled from the ceiling and said, "Janie, your kitchen is not only comfortable but efficient. No wonder everything you make turns out so well."

Janie laughed, "Bets, anybody can grill a hamburger and bake a pie, but thank you."

Doc lit a fire in the family room and everyone relaxed on sofas and cushion chairs. The furniture was not worn, but showed evidence of gentle use. Azi curled up on the bean bag that spread across the living room like the green microscopic organism he had studied in medical school. Saima noticed that one wall was adorned with degrees and awards. She had wondered why Doc did not display these indications of achievement in his office, like so many of his contemporaries. Here they were in a private setting available only for friends and family. That was Doc.

Doc turned to his colleagues and said, "I overheard an interesting conversation in the hospital cafeteria the other day. I am sure they shouldn't share this information, but two of your techs were gabbing about your recent experiment on, as they said, 'how to eliminate death.'"

Alex chuckled. "Mankind will never eliminate death as long as we indulge ourselves in unhealthy diets, smoking, and carcinogens in the pesticides we spray on our lawns to make our grass look pretty and green."

Alex added, " Besides, I've given up the quest to find a way that we can live forever. Aging does not have a single cause. Extending life span is a task of great complexity and difficulty. There are just too many variables. I could never solve them all in my lifetime, no matter how long that will be. The better question is, 'Can we extend our healthy life span a minimum of 50 years?' There are likely hundreds of genes that affect aging and we have only one, our new friend Gene P. We have also discovered the substance that purges tissue of senescent cells. Basically, the essence of dying is our failure to keep our cells healthy. We die because our cells cease to replicate and either die or become senescent. In the next 100 years we will probably be able to zero in on other age agents that can grant us perhaps another 100 years after that, and so on and so on. Death will be eliminated in steps."

Azi went to the kitchen for another piece of pie. He returned and said, "We were correct about one thing: Our study success-fully proved our hypothesis about Gene P's effect on aging."

Alex stood and began to pace, "Azi and I were also successful with our additional experiments behind the radioactive door. You know that fifty extra years I was referring to? We've done it."

Azi winked at Saima. He cautioned, "Many slips between the glass and the mouth."

Doc laughed. "Azi, that's 'There's many a slip twixt the cup and the lip' but hey, that's amazing. Wow!" Doc continued as he raised his lemonade glass. "Congratulations on your efforts and extraordinary achievements so far."

Alex turned to Doc, "Milty, you and Janie are our closest friends. Betsy and I have decided to waste no more time and to arrest our aging as soon as possible. Azi has opted in. Saima is not so sure."

Azi broke in. "Let's be clear, if Saima isn't ready, neither am I."

Doc was alarmed, "Alex, have you proved the safety of this aging antidote of yours? Have you done any advanced animal studies? And weren't you going to do a larger Gene P study of a million samples?"

"Doc, broad animal studies are not appropriate here. There is no time for that. When we solved progeria we did not sacrifice a single dog. Last year, children were dying of progeria—standing on the railroad tracks waiting to be run over. The locomotive was in sight and looming larger.

"Now we are all standing on the railroad tracks. Yes, we're all dying—of old age. Every year that you are alive, your risk of dying increases by 10 percent. That locomotive looms larger for all of us every moment.

"Doc, you studied diabetes—Banting and Best. They successfully extracted insulin and saved thousands of children who were starving to death from the early treatment for type 1 diabetes. That led to the manufacture of insulin by Eli Lilly and Co., saving lives and making a huge fortune for scores of Col. Eli Lilly heirs. The account I read stated that the urgency was deemed so great that Banting suspended the animal studies after ten dogs—just ten dogs. We have the same urgency here."

Doc was soft-spoken in his reply. "Alex, the accounts of the Banting-Best team have been controversial for more than half a century. Banting was awarded the Nobel. Best was not. It was said Best was delusional in his claims. There was bad blood between them. Other scientists claimed to have beaten Banting and Best with insulin. It was a mess. No one knew what to believe, least of all what went on in the lab regarding dog studies."

Alex replied, "Well, I did conduct an animal study—in a way."

Betsy broke her confidence, "He gave it to Mendel."

"Your puppy?"

"Yep, that was last week. Nothing changed. He's still not potty trained."

Doc stared at Alex, "Did you receive FDA clearance to administer your cocktail to dogs?"

"No Milt, I didn't apply for animal studies and I didn't give my therapy to dogs—just my own pet. Mendel is a border collie. Border collies are working dogs. They have a reputation for intelligence, and they are highly motivated. All puppies have a high learning curve, but with maturity the curve flattens out. If I'm right, Mendel will be a puppy for decades. He will be the smartest or most learned dog in the world. He goes to a dog trainer two half-days a week to improve his vocabulary. I just wish I had the time and patience to teach him to his full potential."

Janie said, "You gave this stuff to your own dog?"

"It was after midnight. I was in the lab. You know the Chivas I keep in the cabinet, well …"

Doc nodded to wife. "Take your time, Alex. If you do this right, you'll earn a Nobel Prize." Doc could not hide his concern. "You're going rogue again. Alex, you have no evidence that your theories, whatever they are, will work."

Janie wiped her eyes. "Please Betsy, don't let him do this. There'll be a better time."

Alex shot back, "Would you rather die at 75 with a Nobel Prize clutched in your fist or live twice that long with a chance to win a basketful of Nobels? Time is exactly what we're dealing with. A minute that ticks off is a minute lost. It is the only commodity we can't get back. Time should not be wasted—not a minute—not a second.

"Milt, this really isn't so crazy, and besides, I'm not the first scientist to subject his body to test his theories. What about Walter Reed, who allowed himself to be bitten by a mosquito to prove that malaria was transmitted by a mosquito bite?

"Alex, that was not malaria, it was yellow fever."

Alex was unbowed. "I got the mosquito part right."

"Alex, the story is apocryphal. Okay, if you're going in that direction, what about Dr. Jekyll? He drank his own concoction. Look what happened to him."

"C'mon, Milt. You know that's science fiction. Get real. Scientists ingest their own discoveries all the time. They don't ask permission. Most of the time they don't even tell anyone."

Azi supported Alex. "Although this is a dangerous adventure, I feel very comfortable in what we have accomplished so far. I know what works in a flask and in a mouse is not always effective in the human body. This stuff may not work, but it is not likely to hurt us either. I am living on lended time anyway."

Alex corrected his friend, "borrowed time."

"Cancer cells, like neonatal cells, don't die. But it's very unlikely that what we've discovered would cause cancer. Perhaps, if someone already had cancer, our juice would make it much more difficult to arrest. All in all, the opportunity to live another 50 years is worth the risk, and I don't wish to wait another decade for clinical studies to prove what I am 99 percent certain to be the case."

Milt said, "Alex, I love you like a brother, and I'm going to support whatever you do, no matter how difficult that is for me. I went to bat for you with Marty on your progeria adventure. Poor Jimmy might be dead by now but for your brilliance. Now, the urgency is not so great. Days are precious to us all, but we can spare a few to do this right. Gene tinkering is dangerous and you want to administer this juice of yours to normal people— you and Betsy. Humans have a long history of messing around with Mother Nature, often with unintended consequences. I've always done things by the book, and I will continue to do so. I think Janie is with me on this. We thank you profoundly for this unique opportunity. Today, we choose to die elegantly and naturally and on time, a decision we may come to regret. Let us know when your therapy is proven to be safe, FDA-approved, and available to all."

Janie mused out loud. "I don't know, Milt. Let's keep it in the backs of our minds and for our children and grandchildren. We all want extra tomorrows.

"Who wants more apple pie?"

CHAPTER TWENTY-SIX

A few weeks later Alex hopped into bed. It was after midnight and Betsy was watching Doris Day sing her way through another limp romantic movie on the classic film channel.

"Turn off the TV, Bets. I have an idea." Alex explained his latest revelation. "A number of studies I have read cited the same phenomenon. There is a linkage between fertility and life span. Earthworms and fruit flies—it's the same. We have a calorie-restrictive study underway for Rhesus macaques, but since these monkeys live about three decades, this study will take some patience. It's like what Doc said about fooling Mother Nature. The theory goes that if a species figures out how to extend its life span, then in order to prevent it from flipping a delicate ecological balance, evolution deals it lower fertility and even sterility. But this time we pull a fast one on her. Call it fertility insurance."

Betsy asked, "How do we know what you are about to administer will have that effect on us?"

"We know the juice is a cocktail that will extend our life spans. I believe our bodies will respond to that with a mechanism to switch resources from reproducing to tissue maintenance."

Alex admitted, "I don't really know all this, but why chance it? A couple of guys in the physician's lounge were talking about a company in Chicago that will freeze your sperm for donation later using glycerol and solid carbon dioxide. I checked it out. Think what it means to families who can't get pregnant the old-fashioned way, including guys about to have vasectomies or undergo chemotherapy. It solves the problem of human barrenness. Now think what it means to us. We take the juice. I become sterile—so what—we make a withdrawal from my personal account at a cryobank and boom—we have a family."

Betsy added, "You mean I don't have to have sex with you anymore?" Alex did not laugh.

"Do you mean that?"

Betsy squeezed Alex's thigh, "No."

"We have to do this by appointment. I'll set it up for next Wednesday. We can leave Mendel with your mom and dad. We'll drive to Chicago, stay at the Drake, and make a day of it."

"Great, I'll go shopping."

******

The blue 'Vette did not stop breathing fire until it reached the Dan Ryan Expressway on the outskirts of Chicago. Alex and Betsy checked in at the Drake in the early evening and caught a taxi for Wing Yee in Lincoln Park, not the finest eatery the Windy City had to offer, but Betsy's favorite. They shared egg rolls, three choices from the Cantonese menu, pan-fried noodles, a bottle of wine, and deep-fried ice cream—the meal they remembered from when they sneaked away for a weekend during their senior year at IU.

The Drake boasted old Chicago atmosphere, subdued ambience, and small but workable rooms, featuring a king bed when requested. Alex requested. Betsy packed her silk nightgown with the fur on the bottom. The fur was tickling her chin in less than thirty seconds.

At 10:00 the next morning Betsy reached for Alex's hand as they climbed the steps to the Heaven-Sent Storage Bank. He took it and released it. He put his hand in his pocket—changed his mind and grabbed her hand again. At the top of the stone stairway to the building entrance the block letters read, "A Division of Life Industries."

Alex put his hand back in his pocket and said, "I don't think we need to do this. Actually, I don't want to do this."

Betsy replied, "Well, it was your idea and we have an appointment, so let's just go up and see what they are talking about. If we are going to do it, we are going to do it now. If we wait until we have children to take the juice, instead of being 40 the rest of your life, you'll be in your 50s and die like your grandfather."

Holding hands again, this time to prevent Alex from bolting back down the stairs, they walked through the waiting room and approached the registration desk. There were two women behind the desk, each wearing a nametag. The redhead had breasts that seemed to be fighting to break out of her gray blouse buttoned to the collar. A just-a-little-too-short skirt with matching flats completed the outfit. Betsy noticed that Alex spent a lot of time reading her nametag. Betsy caught it in a glance. It said "Karen." The other employee was a brunette named Donna. She had nice lines and a pleasant face—thought-provoking if you thought about it long enough, but Alex saw her as no match for her colleague.

Alex, caught by Betsy appreciating the tug-of-war behind the gray blouse, commented in a quiet voice, "I'll bet Karen has collected a lot of sperm."

Donna, wearing no expression at all, said to Alex, "If you are here to make a sperm donation, you will need to complete these qualification evaluation forms."

Alex leaned forward and whispered, "Actually, I won't need an evaluation. I like who I am. I just want to stockpile my sperm for later withdrawal."

Donna deadpanned, "Here is a list of our fees and charges, including collecting, cryo services, and storage, as well as an explanation of our cryo technique, a donor profile questionnaire, and a waiver of liability form. You still need to fill these out. Please complete these forms and we'll get you started."

Donna turned to Betsy and said, "Are you here to choose a sperm donor?"

"No, I've got me one of those." Pointing to Alex she added, giggling loudly, "I'm here to give my donor a hand." She giggled again.

At the other end of the desk, Karen was having a vigorous exchange with a broad-shouldered man in his mid-twenties. Other than massive chest and biceps, he was abbreviated: a buzzcut, too-short shorts, and a clinging T-shirt that said, "Da BEARS." At first glance, Betsy estimated him to be about twice as tall as Alex. She listened in.

Karen said "Billy you were here last week."

Billy whined in an accent that Betsy recognized as somewhere around Alabama, "Karen, I can't get paid for doing this in my apartment. My sperm should be in high demand. I'm a stud bull and besides, I need the money. I got cut Tuesday."

Karen put her hand on Billy's bicep. It didn't even get halfway around. She replied, "Maybe you should have spent more time on the practice field instead of playing with that tiger of yours in our consultation room. We can only pay you for one sperm donation per month. I told you that when you were here last week." Billy moved closer and leaned across the desk, "Remember, President Kennedy said, 'Ask what you can do for your country.' Well, I'm trying to populate it."

 Billy noticed Betsy's appraising glance. He swiveled over to her and said, "Ma'am you're here for sperm? For an upcharge I'll be happy to make a direct deposit for you. I'll give it my best shot."

Betsy stared up at him and said, "Keep your zipper up, Skippy." Karen snickered.

Alex looked up from the forms. "Betsy, they are requiring an alternate notification address if they can't reach you or me. Shall I use your parents or mine?"

"Neither. Put Milt in there and mark the box consenting to him receiving copies of all correspondence. He won't ask questions."

Alex went back to the forms. "I put down five feet, seven inches."

"Not on your best day."

He said with a smile, "Are my eyes really blue?"

"Yes dear. Cobalt blue."

Alex handed the forms to Donna and he and Betsy were directed to "Consultation Room A," an enclosure the size of a suburban clothes closet. Two options were offered—recline on a couch or sit in a chair. On a tidy end table, a stack of *Playboy*, *Screw*, and *Hustler* magazines offered extra stimuli—for those who were not fortunate to bring someone like Betsy along.

Donna closed the door and handed Alex a small paper sack. She explained, "There are three vials in this sack. Deposit your ejaculate in each vial and return them in the sack to me." She allowed herself a grin when she said, "Don't worry. You don't have to fill the vials to the top. Just make sure you save something for each vial." She left and closed the door.

Alex turned to Betsy, "Okay, you know what you are here for."

She unzipped his pants and said, "Now where is little Alex?" After a few minutes it was clear she was getting no response. "Hey Alex, this usually works."

Alex said, "Look Betsy, I can't do this in broad daylight—just on cue. Besides didn't I donate last night? I'm going to need more help. I'll tell you what, why don't you take your clothes off?" Betsy roared with laughter. Alex started laughing too. In the waiting room and at the front desk, everyone looked at one another and pretended not to hear the laughter. Now the Morton conversation could be overheard. Betsy said, "I'm not taking off my clothes. I'm not even taking off my hat. I'm going shopping. This is your problem. You created it; you take care of it all by yourself."

Alex pleaded, "C'mon Betsy, don't leave me."

Betsy slipped the wallet out of Alex's pants, extracted a $100 bill, flipped the wallet on the couch and strode out of the room. Over her shoulder she said, "Meet you back at the hotel. Save some of that deposit for later." When she reached the front desk she spoke to Karen, handed her the $100 bill and sauntered out of the waiting room—her heels clicking as she descended the stone steps.

Karen reached back to unloose the ribbon to let her red hair flow down over her shoulders. As she went around the registration desk she said, "Donna, I'll be right back." By the time she had opened the door to Consultation Room A, she had unbuttoned her blouse down to her waist. She said to Alex, curled up in the corner of the couch with his pants around his knees, "Now what seems to be the problem here?"

CHAPTER TWENTY-SEVEN

Betsy gripped Alex's elbow as they crept from the parking lot and up the steps to the entrance of Rosenbaum Hospital. "Look at all those stars, Bets." They embraced on the top step. Azi looked the other way. Betsy said, "The sky is entreating us to do something absolutely scandalous. Let's go for it."

Alex, Betsy, and Azi entered the Rosenbaum Institute on Aging and punched in Betsy's birthday on the lock to the radioactive room. Alex poured a glass of Chivas with lots of ice. Betsy removed her black hooded sweatshirt, took a bottle of red wine from her backpack, and poured herself a tall glass. Azi accepted Alex's offer of scotch and all three clinked their glasses. Azi placed their IVs.

Betsy took a long draught from her wine and said to Azi, "What exactly is in this stuff I'm getting anyway?"

Azi replied, "Well, you know it's Gene P delivered through an adenoviruses vector, and we added our secret sauce."

"Secret sauce?"

Azi started laughing again.

Alex turned to his wife and said, "You don't want to know."

Betsy, tipsy said, "It's sperm, isn't it? You have called it your secret sauce before."

Azi could not stop laughing.

Alex said, "Well, you don't have to swallow it."

Betsy retorted, "Don't act like I have a problem with sperm. I swallow. Azi, my cells should already have me covered for three hundred years considering how many times I've swallowed."

Azi, becoming noticeably uncomfortable, didn't look at Betsy as he combined the spermidine with the Gene P solution. Alex asked him to wait. He said, "We're going to do this at midnight because it's historic and deserves to have an historic hour."

Azi replied, "Well didn't a lot of bad things happen at midnight? Look what happened to Cinderella's carriage. Maybe that's a bad omen."

Azi, you've been reading too many fairy tales. It's midnight, let's get started."

Betsy looked at the men and said, "Wait a minute. I'm going first."

Alex nodded and activated Betsy's IV. He watched while the solution trickled into Betsy's veins. Azi quickly proceeded to minister to Alex who yelled, "Geronimo!"

Azi said, "Geronimo? That is the name of the barbeque joint next to the NYC Immigration Center."

Alex said, "Drink your scotch, Azi. I'll tell you all about that later." He added, "Azi, we have plenty of juice if you want to change your mind tonight."

Azi shook his head, "Based upon everything we've done in this lab, I know the juice is going to be safe, and I have a feeling that it is very likely to work. All of our hunches, including our work on progeria, have proved to be valid. But as we said, Saima and I are going to wait. We have a few years to play with and we'll use that time to learn from your experiences and perhaps even improve the therapy. We all know that time is precious. Saima and I will not waste any of that commodity."

Azi jotted down midnight April 1, 1980, and noted the dosage in his lab notes. Following his usual procedure, he made a copy to send to attorney Wexler for the lab's confidential backup files and locked the originals in the middle drawer of his desk behind the radioactive door.

When the transfusions were complete, Alex replenished the glasses. Alex, Azi, and Betsy toasted to the occasion. Azi said,

"To my dear and courageous friends. May they be rewarded with a long and happy life."

Alex turned to Betsy and said, "May my remarkable wife be the first person on this planet to live a healthy and vigorous life of at least 150 years."

They drained their glasses and flung them against the large cylindrical container across the room, where they shattered into hundreds of twinkling pieces.

CHAPTER TWENTY-EIGHT

Yosso answered another call from Teddi Colson. He was expecting it. "Ward, I need another consultation. How about Wednesday afternoon?"

"Teddi, Wednesday afternoon is my day off."

"Precisely. It's Marty's day off too. He'll be on the golf course. If it's not raining, how about my house at 2:00?"

Teddi met Yosso at the door in a red jumpsuit that accented the blond hair hanging over her shoulders. The jumpsuit had one silver zipper that went from collar to crotch. "Come on in, Ward, and make yourself comfortable." She led him to the bedroom, where she helped him remove his clothing. Teddi's bed was elevated—majestic. One didn't just lie down but rather climbed up. Yosso knew it would be worth the effort.

She took his finger and put it in the zipper loop. He needed no more instructions. When the zipper reached its destination, the jumpsuit was gone. Teddi said, "Do you remember what you said to me in the examining room? Well, it's your turn. Lie back and make yourself comfortable." She placed a pillow under his lower back and sat between his legs. She anointed her finger with K-Y Jelly and inserted it inside Yosso gently prodding his prostrate. She pressed her other hand against his male parts and said, "Can you feel that?"

"Holy shit! No wonder Marty is always smiling."

"Yes, doctor I feel that." His erection was hard and pulsating. She removed her hands and mounted him with a fury.

He yelled, "Yes, doctor" as they climaxed together.

Yosso lay back on the bed as Teddi went into the bathroom. He thought, "I've had affairs with patients and nurses, but nothing like this. This is better than that first time in my examining room thirty years ago. That was thrilling, but nothing like this. What was the name of that Asian girl?" He turned his head and noticed a folder on the night table. It bore a title in large capital letters, "INVESTIGATION OF THE EFFECT OF NORMAL FIRST CHROMOSOME GENE P ON LAMIN A." Just below the title it said, "Final report submitted by Ralph Jessup, M.D., Co-Investigator." Yosso opened the file and slid out the first two pages that read, Confidential Executive Summary, closed the file, and put it back on the table. He folded the two pages twice, leaned over to the floor, and slipped the folded pages inside his pants pocket.

Teddi returned to the bedroom. Yosso gaped at Teddi in her nakedness as she climbed onto her bed. He sensed motion between his legs. He reached down just to make sure. He said to himself, "This hasn't happened since I was 40." He stroked Teddi's breasts and said, "Wednesday afternoons with you, Teddi, are going to ruin my handicap." Teddi laid her head on Yosso's shoulder. She caressed his smooth scalp and then put her arm across his chest and smiled. "By the way, these last couple of years, sex with Marty has never been better." Yosso went limp.

******

At 4:00 that afternoon, Yosso woke from a nap, put on slippers, and padded into his library. He leaned back in his leather chair and unfolded the purloined executive report. Yosso found little reason to peruse the summary, which included the identification of the principals and their titles, the budget, and a recognition and note of thanks to Bob Block. The summary also stated that the duration of the investigation was ninety days and referred the reader to various appendices in the report that set forth basic data, including the number of samples in each cohort, the form of consent, and a record of interim reports. Yosso read the conclusion in the middle of the second page. "This study successfully demonstrates that Gene P manifests a deterioration of positive effect on lamin A in older cohorts. Its apparent positive influence on most data points wanes, particularly as it relates to the nuclear membrane."

Yosso's eyes settled on the handwritten note at the end of the confidential executive summary. He noted with pleasure that the Jester's script was more legible than his own.

Marty, I was pleased to participate in this study. Thank you for the honor. Alex is brilliant. His experiments are bold and his discoveries are breathtaking.

Alex's irrational behavior in the progeria episode threatened to ruin us all, including our beloved hospital. I'm afraid he's at it again. The preliminary success in this investigation proved his hypothesis about Gene P, and the word around his lab is that cellular experiments he and Azi are conducting behind his "RADIATION DOOR" confirm the hypothesis that replacing a normally aged Gene P with a fresh copy retards aging of the cell lines. If the hypothesis holds up in large studies and carefully prescribed human trials, he may have discovered another boon to mankind.

Marty, Alex isn't going to wait for any of that. It is my reasonable belief that Alex has administered his therapy to himself (he calls it the juice) or will begin soon. I also don't know whether his chief researcher, Azi Dansinghani, and their wives are participants.

Alex has often said when discussing his progeria breakthrough, "Every day lost is a day you never get back." I know that's no reason to break the rules, but the stakes are high. If offered the chance, would I personally consider the juice? Would you?

I'm frightened for Alex. I'm frightened for us all.
Ralph

Yosso placed the report in the bottom desk drawer under a legal pad. He had an idea.

CHAPTER TWENTY-NINE

At seven a.m. on Sunday morning Alex answered the telephone by his bedside. It was Azi. "We had a break-in last night at the lab."

"Was anything damaged or stolen?"

"Not that I can tell exactly, but it does appear that some of our Gene P vials are missing. We can check that with the techs on Monday morning. I'm cleaning up the mess right now."

Alex said, "Azi, what are you doing there bright and early on a Sunday morning?"

Azi replied, "I was sorting and packing. It's a bit sad for me, and I didn't want to do it while everyone was here."

"Okay, Azi, give me time to get dressed. I'll be in, in just a few minutes."

Azi met Alex at the door. "Look what I found?"

"What is it?"

"It's a candy wrapper. I found it on the floor over there by the file cabinets."

"Aha! The Jester, we should have expected this. Well, we can't just accuse him outright. He'll deny it, and we won't get anywhere."

Azi suggested, "We could call the police and ask for an investigation—fingerprints and all that. That would be a bad idea, though, in light of what we're doing up here."

"I agree, Azi, but we do need to send a confidential memo to our colleagues. They'll probably find out anyway, and maybe it will prod the Jester to incriminate himself."

On Monday morning the following report was sent to investigative study members, with a copy to Marty Colson.

MEMORANDUM

To: Investigative Study Members
From: Azayiz Dansinghani, M.D.
Co-Lead Investigator

It is my unfortunate duty to report to you that last Saturday night the Institute on Aging was the object of a burglary. Although we are still investigating, we know that none of the Study Commission data has been compromised. We have confirmed, however, that some of our vials of Gene P are missing.

Gene P on its own is of little value and can be replicated here in the lab. Follow-up research to our successful study has shown that Gene P is relatively ineffective on aging processes without its combination with certain enzymes that we have identified. Various combinations of those enzymes with Gene P are under investigation to determine the solutions' effect on the aging process. We have always stored the enzyme solutions separately and only combined them with Gene P just before each experiment began.

We believe the break-in was not a random act of vandalism, but a direct assault on the important work that is taking place at the institute. In response we have stored the enzyme solutions in the room normally reserved for experiments with radioactive materials.

If you learn any information regarding this unfortunate incident, please let us know.

Alex said to Azi, "I think this should smoke him out, and I bet he'll come on Saturday night just like last week."

Azi replied, "I'll sleep in the lab Saturday night, but why smoke? Do we have to light a fire?"

Alex shrugged his shoulders and stared at Azi.

"Wait a moment. I think I get that one."

Saturday night came and went without incident. At daylight, Azi awoke from a fitful sleep at his desk and went home to take a nap.

Azi and Alex talked on Monday morning. Alex said, "Perhaps we haven't given him enough rope. Mendel and I will stay here for a few nights and see if we can catch him."

******

The following Saturday night, Alex was awakened from a light slumber on his office couch by a soft sound from the back of Mendel's throat. Alex rose and lifted the Indianapolis Racers hockey stick from its hook on the wall. He whispered, "Mendel, silence." Mendel and Alex listened to light steps followed by click, click, click as the tumblers turned on the lock of the radioactive door. When the door opened, Alex struck the intruder across the back with the hockey stick and exclaimed, "Aha! Jester, we've caught you like a rat in a trap." The intruder groaned, dropped the flashlight and fell to the floor. The hockey stick fell to the floor at the same time—in two pieces.

Alex seized the flashlight. He blinked as he tried to focus his eyes around the halo of light in the dark room. The burglar, clad in black pants, jacket, and ski mask, stood and groaned again in a high pitch. Alex gasped. It was not the Jester.

CHAPTER THIRTY

Alex beckoned with his flashlight. "Take off your jacket and hat and make yourself at home." He turned on a lamp and watched the intruder let loose hair from the ski hat that had been pulled down—long blond hair descended over *her* shoulders.

"Teddi Colson, what are you doing here at this hour? I would apologize for the hockey stick but I don't believe an apology from *me* is in order. I'm embarrassed for you."

"I know what you are up to, Alex, and I want to play too." Teddi started to cry.

"How much does Marty know about this escapade of yours?"

"Nothing, Alex, I swear. He is only guilty of bringing his files home and leaving them on the night table. At first, I read the reports out of curiosity, but then I became convinced in light of your track record that you and your friends have found a way to live forever. I am one of your friends, aren't I?"

"You were until I caught you in my lab in the middle of the night. And what makes you think you could prepare our age therapy and properly administer it anyway?"

"I'm an experienced nurse. That's child's play. You're not fooling anybody, Alex. According to one memo in Marty's file, you may have already administered the wonder drug to yourself. Can you deny that?"

"Look, Teddi, we are still in an experimental stage. Suppose we forget about this episode and I promise to include you and Marty in our first FDA study."

"Alex, please, that may be too late for me. I'm almost fifty years old. I can't afford to age another day."

"You are barely forty. Go on home, Teddi. Keep this matter entirely to yourself. Don't even mention it to Marty. We'll talk in a week or two."

Teddi said, "Thank you." She hugged Alex with a full contact embrace. When Alex didn't resist, she found his lips with a lingering kiss. Mendel leaped from the couch and snarled at her feet. Alex separated from Teddi's clutches, walked her to the elevator, and pushed the down button.

The next morning Azi and Alex discussed the situation.

"Alex, can we trust Mrs. Colson to keep her mouth shut and stay out of our lab?"

"I think so. I'll discuss it with her after I give the matter a couple of weeks to cool down."

"So, it wasn't the Jester. I was so sure."

"No, Azi, it wasn't the Jester after all. We convicted him on the basis of one discarded candy wrapper. I feel like I owe him an apology."

CHAPTER THIRTY-ONE

"I am pregnant!"

Alex had just entered the house after parking his Corvette in the garage. He rushed into the kitchen and found Betsy in a red apron holding a carving knife and fork in her hands. Both utensils clattered to the floor as Betsy welcomed Alex's gentle hug.

"Are you sure? I thought this would never happen. We're over forty, you know."

"Well, we don't kill rabbits anymore, but yes, Dr. Patterson and I are sure. I am so sure that we've invited your parents and mine for dinner tonight. I'll let you make the announcement. Now go clean up. Our moms will be over in a few minutes to help me with the cooking."

When Betsy came into the marriage, her culinary skills were limited to lasagna and bacon, lettuce, and tomato sandwiches. She announced to Alex, "Tonight's menu is lamb chops, medium rare, a corn souffle, and a salad. And for that, I emptied every can in our pantry into a mixing bowl, including mandarin oranges, artichoke hearts, and hearts of palm. Mom is bringing over your favorite dessert, cherry pie, and I have some ice cream in the freezer."

"Oh, and Alex, before you go, chill some champagne from the liquor closet. Grab that bottle of Roederer Estate, the one we got from the Dansinghanis when they were over for dinner last month."

The mothers came over in one car, Emily's new black Mercedes sedan. Tina turned a knowing eye to Emily. "Well, a baby is finally on the way."

Emily showed no surprise. "Did Betsy tell you?"

"No."

"She didn't tell me either. I know you're right." Tina dabbed at her eyes. My first grandchild. Kevin may even take a puff from one of Logan's cigars."

When they greeted Betsy, she was bursting with her important news, but was able to keep what she thought was her secret.

In the kitchen, Emily noticed the writing on Betsy's red apron. It said in a lively script, "Come and get it."

"Where did you find that apron, Betsy?"

"Actually, Mom, it was a gift from my sorority sister, Sally Henry."

Tina chimed in. "You mean 'No Pants' Henry?"

"Does Alex tell you everything? Sally gave me the apron more than a dozen years ago after what she described as a horrendous experience while wearing it one night at a cookout at the Sigma Nu fraternity house."

As the guests seated themselves for dinner, Alex filled their glasses. The dining room table was deep walnut and could seat fourteen. It was a house gift from the moms and dads. The Howells bought the table and the Mortons bought the chairs. In the eight years Betsy and Alex lived in their home, this was the first time they formally "dined."

Betsy said, "Alex would like to make an announcement."

Alex raised his glass and began, "Eh, uh, er."

Betsy blurted out, "I'm pregnant!"

Alex recovered with, "We're pregnant! So, let's raise our glasses to Betsy and the new member of our family."

Kevin let out a big whoop and holler. Mendel was awakened from his nap in the den and trotted into the room. He was rewarded with pats of affection from everyone.

Betsy drained her glass and said, "That's the last alcohol I will consume until we have our baby."

Betsy monopolized the dinner conversation with information about her trips to the doctor and how she was feeling. Logan inquired, "Boy or girl?"

Betsy giggled. She said, "You know Alex. He's a scientist with a scientist's curiosity. He's got to know everything. Alex?"

"Tomorrow I'll run a sample of Betsy's tissues through our DNA testing equipment. Betsy's DNA and that of the baby is in her bloodstream. If we do not detect male chromosomes, it's a girl."

After dessert, Logan offered Kevin one of his Cuban cigars. Before they could light up, Betsy stared at them and said, "Dad, please no smoking." The three men went out to the porch while the two mothers relaxed around the dinner table and regaled Betsy with details of their pregnancies.

Alex turned to his father and father-in-law and said, "I heard you guys recently garnered a big award."

Logan sat up in his chair, took a puff of his cigar and said, "Yes, we were proud to receive the Kaiser Award recognizing our achievement as a leader in global wholesale used vehicle sales. We reached our goal of the sale of 3 million vehicles last year. We are now in more than fifty locations across North America and Europe. Your dad and I are a great team."

Kevin changed the subject, "What's the proud father-to-be up to these days?"

Logan added, "Is all that trouble over with at Rosenbaum?"

Alex nodded, "My hospital privileges have been fully restored. In fact, Marty Colson is quite pleased over the new prominence of Rosenbaum Children's Hospital, due in no small part to the article my friend Tom Harton wrote about me in *Indianapolis Business Journal*. It was picked up by the national press. The CFO, Rosanne Ross, announced donations are up and I've signed a new contract Wexler prepared that raises my salary to more than $100,000, including benefits, and grants me a 50 percent interest in any proprietary rights that are developed out of the Institute on Aging. In addition, we've earned a number of grants, and the good thing is that most are open-ended, so I can pursue pure research in any direction that takes me."

Alex's father let out a long whistle. "Wow, that's a lot of carburetors."

Logan said, "Carburetors?"

"Yeah, my grandfather, who established our repair garage, used to get two bits per carburetor and when he heard about someone having a lot of money that was one of his favorite expressions."

Logan took another puff, "Alex, are you sure you're not wasting time on this aging thing?"

"No, Logan. If we fall short on our quest to live forever, there is still much progress we can make. Some of our discoveries may help with cures for dementia, cancer, and other diseases associated with our failing bodies. It's an exploding field with plenty of opportunity, and right now Azi and I and the others on our team are very excited about some new experiments. But it's frustrating.

"Ever since I presented that paper at the Progeria Research Foundation, about 20 percent of my time is spent fielding inquiries from doctors around the world. I take care of my progeria consulting practice every Monday, and I devote the rest of my time to the institute's quest to extend the human life span. On Monday, I am a hero all day long and beloved by people who seek my advice and want to congratulate and award me, but the rest of the week I am just another one of a growing army of scientists trying to race against Mother Nature. Until recently, we were all tied for last. Now, Azi and I have some breakthroughs that have not been published."

Alex felt like an Olympic sprinter about to break the tape with no one in the stands. Betsy had forbidden him to discuss their "adventure" with family.

Logan said, "If you try to explain one of your theories to me, will I be able to understand it?"

"Let me try. We know that aging is controlled by a genetic process. The major evidence in support of this theory derived from the species specificity of maximum life span. Variation of life span is far greater among species than within species. For example, our species lives about 70 years. Octopuses live about one year. Because maximum life span is a species characteristic, it must be genetically determined. Our research with progeria has proved the theory conclusively. We defeated progeria by isolating what we call Gene P. Gene P is a gene on the number one chromosome that, when defective, causes the proteins of the cell to break down and the cell to die. We were able to isolate Gene P by comparing the samples from our progeria patients with samples of healthy Gene P and effectively replace that gene with a healthy gene. That's all history.

"Our premise now is that perhaps the normal iteration of Gene P begins to mutate over the course of years or in some other way becomes less effective at stabilizing the nucleus in the cell, causing it to die or lapse into what we call senescence, which is about as bad. To put it another way, the defective Gene P accelerated aging in progeria patients. Perhaps the normal Gene P affects aging in the normal course. What if progeria is just normal aging at a faster pace? What if we could slow down the effects of the Gene P deterioration and keep our cells alive and healthy, if not forever, for many more years?"

Kevin leaned back in his chair and said, "Wow, that sure makes sense to me."

Alex continued, "It's the theory we are most excited about today, but we have catalogued more than 100 separate theories on why our bodies age."

Logan said, "I remember the theory my mother told me. She was trying to deter my frantic activity. I remember she said, 'Live fast and die young.' She compared the mouse we found scurrying back and forth in the kitchen to my pet turtle that barely moved. She said the life span of the mouse was measured in months and the turtle would live hundreds of years."

Alex asked, "Did you believe her theory?"

"No."

"Why not?"

"My turtle died a week later."

"Logan, the secret to the long life of a turtle does not lie with its lethargic behavior. It is because its cells can divide more than twice as many times as human cells before becoming aged."

"Alex, if I can be of any assistance with further funding of your lab, please let me know."

Alex responded, "Actually Logan, it's been grand at Rosenbaum with all the recognition. I put the arm on Marty to buy us a couple more sophisticated machines that we couldn't afford in our original budget. With all that comes more responsibilities as our hospital has garnered more respect on the world stage."

Alex refilled their glasses and stood up. "Gentlemen, I propose a toast to your new grandchild. May this baby live 1,000 years."

CHAPTER THIRTY-TWO

Alex was an early riser. He did not use an alarm clock to wake up at six. The morning after the big announcement, Alex popped out of bed at five. He dressed in the darkness so as not to disturb his wife and their precious new package. He bounded up the steps to Rosenbaum's sixth floor with Betsy's tissue sample that had been carefully collected and preserved in their home freezer. It took eleven minutes for the DNA analyzer to spit out the results of the tissue screen. Alex didn't bother with the details. He made a quick observation. There was no sign of male DNA. He yelled out to the empty room, "It's a girl!"

Later than morning he thrust the results under Azi's nose. "It's a girl! It's a girl!"

Azi was more careful in his analysis of the report. "You read it just right. I'm excited for you, but Alex, take a closer look at this analysis. The report shows the presence of telomerase. This enzyme should not be present in a normal DNA scan. I'm not sure, but I wouldn't expect pregnancy to promote the production of telomerase."

Alex's grin vanished. He had more experience with oncology and had a better idea of what he was looking at. "You are right, Azi. Betsy needs to see Dr. Patterson for a thorough investigation, including an examination for possible cancer."

******

Dr. Patterson discovered lesions on Betsy's ovaries. Lab tests came back positive for ovarian cancer. Dr. Patterson met with

Betsy and Alex in his office. She said, "Alex, thanks to your suspicions, we were able to diagnose the cancer at stage I. That is, the lesions are confined to the inside of your ovaries, Betsy, and not extended to the basement membrane. About one in every 1,000 pregnant women are diagnosed with some form of cancer. Ovarian cancer with pregnancy is more rare. Because the uterus blocks the ovaries, we probably would not have picked up this diagnosis. Most ovarian cancer is commonly detected in stage III or IV, when it is very often too late. There's a very good chance we will be able to cure you."

Betsy said, "What about my baby?"

Dr. Patterson folded her hands on her lap. "Yes, you might suffer a miscarriage. The closer your lesions are to your uterus, the more likely that will occur. It's probable we can save you both. Ovarian cancer is a deadly disease, but when diagnosed early it can be beaten. We'll need to start you on therapy right away. Let's schedule surgery within a month."

One month later the presurgical diagnosis was not so good. "Betsy," began Dr. Patterson, "your cancer has taken an unexpected turn and has progressed to stage III. Comparative X-rays of your tumors show rapid growth, and they are no longer confined to the inside of your ovaries. I have never seen an ovarian cancer this aggressive. In order to save your life, we're going to have to take the baby. We're going to do a radical hysterectomy."

Betsy said, "Can't we wait six months and do it at that time after I deliver?"

"You are the patient, Betsy, but I wouldn't recommend it."

Betsy sobbed. "It's that damn juice of yours, Alex. I love you, but you lost our baby and I think you've killed me."

Alex held Betsy and whispered, "Let's go home and we can continue that conversation later." After they left, Dr. Patterson began sobbing as well. That evening they lay in bed and held one another as Alex tried to explain, "Betsy, we had no idea the juice would cause your cancer. Embryonic cells are primed for rapid growth and sometimes, somehow, they become uncontrollable.

The juice may have triggered that. Let's beat this thing together, and we'll figure another way to have as many children as you want."

The next day Alex and Azi sat down to discuss Betsy's situation. They came to the same conclusion. The senescent cells that they removed had played a fundamental role as a governor to retard the growth of neonatal cells. Without that governor, the cell division had run amok and turned cancerous.

Azi lamented to Alex, "We caused Betsy's cancer, and we will cause her death."

Alex pleaded, "Suppose they give her a radical hysterectomy and stave off ovarian cancer long enough for the senescent cells to materialize."

Azi said, "It's just not possible. Senescent cells won't appear fast enough to keep up with the devastation caused by these out-of-control neonatal cells, now turned deadly cancerous. You've studied oncology. You and I both know all existing therapies will be inadequate in defense of this storm. You might think there is a chance for Betsy if we take the baby and perform a radical hysterectomy. The problem is that by the time we go to surgery, even tomorrow, there is no chance. The cancer has metastasized. In stage IV, that protocol will do us no good."

"Go home, Alex. Take a leave of absence. Spend as much quality time with Betsy as possible. Don't worry about anything else. I'll take care of the lab."

Alex cupped the top of his head with his hands. "You know I can't take a leave of absence. We saved Jimmy. We have to figure out how to save Betsy and our baby girl. The answers will be here in the lab." Azi knew there would be no time left for that. He put his hand on Alex's shoulder as he walked him to the door.

CHAPTER THIRTY-THREE

"Hey, Alex, it's Yos. Are you going to be in your lab later on this afternoon or early evening? I have to go over to Rosenbaum anyway and I can drop that foreskin tissue by if you are going to be around."

Alex replied, "I need to be home by 7:30, but I have plenty to do in my lab until then."

"Okay Alex, that will be fine. I'll see you around 6:30."

Alex put down the telephone and yelled to Azi, "If you can stay a little late tonight, Yosso is coming by with those specimens we need."

At 6:30 Yosso entered the Institute on Aging with a package. He walked through the laboratory and noticed that the radioactive door was slightly open. He had never been invited to explore that part of the laboratory, so he took advantage of the opportunity. Alex heard the tap, tap, tap of a cane. He looked up from his microscope and said, "Yos, welcome. Come on in." He then arose, went out the door and asked Azi to join them.

"Azi, please take Dr. Yosso's package and put it in our storage unit."

Azi said, "Dr. Yosso, it is a pleasure to see you, and thank you again for helping us with our research."

Azi left the room while Alex and Yosso sat down. Yosso rubbed his hand over his smooth scalp. He pulled on his chin, then he stood up and put his hands in his pockets.

Alex implored, "Please sit down and relax."

Yosso sat down and said, "How's Betsy?"

Alex replied, "Well, as you and all our friends know, Betsy is struggling with her cancer. I wouldn't share this with everyone, but she's not going to make it. We have already lost our baby."

Yosso shook his head. "I heard all this from Patterson. I am so sorry, Alex."

Alex took out his handkerchief and said, "How's Melanie?"

"I don't know. Mel and I broke up a couple of weeks ago. I moved out. Nobody really knows that yet."

"I'm sorry to hear that, Yos."

"Well, that's okay. Carolyn and I have been seeing one another for a long time and Melanie finally booted me."

"Who's Carolyn?"

"You remember Carolyn. She's the nurse, the redheaded one in my office. I've been a sucker for redheads all my life. I've been staying at her place. She is visiting her kids for the next two weeks so I am 'baching' it. We're making plans. I retired from my practice and I'm moving to Cuernavaca with Carolyn as soon as possible. It is dubbed, "City of Eternal Spring." There are lots of ex-pats down there. Carolyn is "mi amor grande." She can make love in three languages. I won't be missed in Indy. Patterson has taken over as practice manager. Alex, how's your research coming along?

"Wow, that's a lot. We're doing okay, Yos, but I ..."

"Alex, I want the juice. Now more than ever. If things don't work out with Carolyn, I'm back on the market. I need the juice— and if they do work out, well, she'll need the juice too."

"What juice? I don't know what you're talking about."

"I read the Jester's report. I know it's confidential. It's not Marty's fault, but I happened to see it and Patterson told me about your appointment. I know you are taking the juice, and I know you gave it to Betsy. I've been your partner on this research by supplying all the material that you needed and you owe me. I can keep a secret."

Alex stood up. "I don't owe you anything, Yos, just because you supplied me with a bunch of lousy foreskins. Besides, I can't disseminate something you're calling 'the juice.' It's a violation of FDA rules. You know that."

Yosso stood and faced Alex. He raised his voice and thrust a finger in Alex's face. "Look, I have a proposition for you. You let me have the juice just like you are taking it, for say, twenty years. I'll disappear with Carolyn and won't bother you. If you don't accept this proposition, I'm going to take the Jester's confidential report, add my scientific conclusion based on Betsy's situation, and provide that information to the Marion County Prosecutor. He will engage in an investigation. I'll suggest the prosecutor subpoena Wexler's files, which I understand will contain the entire sordid story." Yosso lifted his cane. "Your hospital privileges will be revoked, and your career will be wrecked. You'll bring down the hospital, and if Betsy dies, which we both know she will, you will be convicted of murder and thrown in the clink forever. You killed Betsy. I think I know how. Basically, Alex you give me the juice or I'll ruin you."

Alex heard a loud pop and saw Yosso fall to his knees and then forward, hitting his face on the table. Yosso rolled over and landed on his back with his mouth agape and a hole the size of a silver dollar in his forehead. Alex looked down. His lab coat was splattered with bits of bone, blood, and brain tissue. Azi whimpered as he stood with his pistol in his right hand and groaned at Alex, "Aye khudha, yeh kya ho gaya!"

Alex replied, "Azi, I don't know what you just said, but I agree with you 100 percent."

Alex was distraught, but he held his emotions in order not to further traumatize Azi. He put his arm around his friend's shoulder and said, "Azi, you're pretty good with that pop gun, aren't you? I'm not sure this was a good idea, but Azi, we do have to get rid of Yosso and we don't have enough piranhas. Let me have your pistol. I'll dispose of that for you. Now relax. Go out into the lab and bring me the step stool and a bucket—oh, and two pairs of cryogenic gloves."

Alex drained some of the liquid nitrogen from the bottom of the large cylindrical cyber tank, unscrewed the top and beckoned

Azi to help him remove the two Rhesus monkeys. They placed one in a tank in the outer laboratory. Alex looked toward Yosso. "Azi, lift the dead meat and lean it on the tank."

Azi breathed fast and deep. "I can't. He's too heavy."

"Ok, I'll do that." Alex raised Yosso by the shoulders and dragged him up the step stool. He leaned the inert mass on the tank with its head just over the rim.

"Now, Azi, lift Yosso's feet, and we'll give him his last bath." Together they plunged Yosso headfirst into the cylinder. He made a loud hiss as his body slid into the tank.

"Azi, you want this fancy cane as a memento of the occasion?"

Azi couldn't speak. Alex slipped the cane in the tank and watched the cobra dip below the surface of the liquid nitrogen. They set the second Rhesus monkey back in the tank on top of Yosso. There was just enough room for Alex's soiled lab coat. After Alex replaced the top, he turned to Azi and said, "Now, let's scrub the blood stain out of the carpet." Azi did not respond.

Azi's whimper turned to a wail. After Alex cleaned the carpet, he walked Azi to his car. Alex spilled the whole story to Betsy that night.

She said, "Yosso was a rat. I feel sorry for Azi. My dear Alex, you did the right thing."

"Maybe I did the right thing for the wrong reasons."

CHAPTER THIRTY-FOUR

Azi, in the passenger seat of Alex's Corvette, turned to his friend and said, "You shouldn't have left Betsy's bedside. Thank you so much. I will miss you, Alex. I hope we have more opportunities to work together."

Alex replied, "Don't dwell on that incident of last week, Azi. There are great things ahead for you. I will look after Saima until she and Faraz join you after his school year. Oh, and by the way, I have two gifts for you. You may open the one in red wrapping paper any time you wish. Pack the one in the blue package in your suitcase before you board the plane. It is American-made. I hope you never need it."

"Thank you, Alex." Azi packed the blue package in his suitcase and turned to wave to Alex as he entered the terminal. In the passenger lounge he ripped open the red paper wrapping and extracted his gift. It was a hardbound book titled, "A Treasure of American Idioms," which Alex had inscribed: "To Azi, A friendship like ours comes along 'once in a blue moon.' We are 'two peas in a pod.' Alex."

Alex roared down the airport ramp and onto the highway. He rememberd that Betsy warned him to decelerate when he reached their neighborhood. The Howell men—Logan, Louis, and Liam—sat in the corner of the living room. Their wives sat with Emily Howell in another corner, dabbing their eyes with tissues and whispering. Kevin sat in a rocking chair next to Logan. The two of them always talked business, but not today. Alex hugged his father, then rushed down the back hall. He was met at the bedroom door by the home hospice nurse.

"How's Betsy doing?"

"She's awake mostly but drifting in and out. She's complaining about her cold feet. I put on some thick warm hospital socks."

"Thank you. Uh, er, I'm sorry. I have forgotten your name."

From the bedroom Betsy's mother said, "It's Mildred."

"That's right. I remember now. Thank you, Mildred."

Alex sat next to Mendel at the end of the bed. He removed Betsy's socks and massaged her feet. He noticed they were tinged in purple and blue. He looked down the bed to Betsy and said, "Are you hungry?"

Betsy shook her head. "This is not the journey you promised me."

"Betsy, are you in pain?"

"No, no pain."

Mildred said to Alex, "She is on a morphine protocol." Mildred held up a vial smaller than a nail polish bottle. "This contains ten milligrams of highly concentrated medicine called hydromorphone. We are dosing her between her lower lip and her teeth, two milligrams every six hours. I have just given her a dose. She will not suffer any pain."

Alex beckoned the mothers to join him in the living room. He addressed his family. "Thank you for being with us during this dreadful episode. I'm going to have some private time with Betsy while we still can, so please go on home and do come back tomorrow." Alex went back into the bedroom. Mildred had put the hospital socks back on Betsy's feet.

"Mildred, it might be a good time for you to get some dinner. Mendel and I will be right by Betsy's bedside until you return."

Mildred rose from her chair and handed Alex her card. "Here is my emergency telephone number. I'll only be ten minutes away."

When she left, Alex lay down in bed next to Betsy. She turned to Alex and said, "Do I have a chance, Alex?"

"No, Bets."

"I've been thinking about the first time we made love."

"Keep that in your thoughts, Bets."

"Oh, Alex, I love you. Dying is hard work."

"I know, Bets. I'm not going to leave you."

Betsy whispered, "We were going to live forever."

Alex sobbed, "You will live forever in my thoughts and in my dreams."

Alex wiped a tear from her eye. She reached up and squeezed his hand.

"Okay, Alex, I'm ready to go."

Alex took the ten-milligram bottle of hydromorphone and filled the dropper with two milligrams. He pulled back Betsy's bottom lip and deposited the contents of the dropper.

Betsy sighed, "I'm cold. Please get our special blanket, the one with the blue and pink flower buds."

Alex wrapped Betsy in the blanket. He refilled the dropper and deposited two more milligrams. "Are you warmer now?"

"No, please hold me, Alex. I hear crickets."

Alex administered yet another dose of the hydromorphone. "Betsy?"

Betsy was unresponsive.

Alex delivered the last dose with the dropper and put the empty bottle in his pocket. He climbed in bed next to Betsy and held her close in his arms. He cried himself to sleep.

An hour later Alex woke to Mildred's gentle tapping. "Dr. Morton, Dr. Morton! Please wake up! Your wife has passed."

CHAPTER THIRTY-FIVE

"Hey Boss. Did you get one of these?" Alex picked up the letter that Hilary slid across his desk.

Before he glanced at it, he said to Hilary, "Don't know, I haven't read my personal mail in a couple of months."

Hilary responded, "Put it all in a sack and bring it in. Let me tell you what this says. It's a letter from a grand jury 'inviting' my testimony in an investigation regarding Betsy's death."

"Uh-oh. I'll go home at lunch and bring you the sack."

That afternoon Hilary helped Alex trash most of his mail. They kept the grand jury letter. Alex called Wexler, "David, we need to talk. Do you have some time later today?"

Alex couldn't recall being in David Wexler's office, despite years of representation. They did business by telephone or at the hospital. Alex wondered how Wexler could do any business at all. His desk was piled with books and papers. Like a mud flow they oozed across the floor and onto tables and chairs. Alex sat down in a side chair while Wexler walked around his desk, removed folders from another chair and placed them in a pile on the floor. He leaned back in the chair, stretched his long legs and placed his feet on the document pile he had displaced. Clerks, assistants, and secretaries walked about his office placing items in his inbox, removing papers from his outbox and plopping materials on his desk. Phones rang, buzzers buzzed.

Wexler said, "Alex, what a pleasure to see you. It seems forever since we've had some quiet time to talk."

Alex looked around, "Quiet time?"

Wexler got up and closed the door. "What's the matter, Alex?"

"This came in the mail for me."

Wexler glanced at the letter. He read:

Dear Dr. Morton,

This letter and the enclosed target subpoena will serve as official notification that a Marion County grand jury is presently investigating the death of Betsy Morton and you are a target of this investigation.

He did not need to read the remainder of the letter. He had seen these before. "Well Alex, you are a target of a Marion County grand jury investigation. Many people will be non-targets, like your assistant, Hilary Stout. They may be asked to testify as well. I did not receive a letter, but I might due to my association with Rosenbaum." Wexler reached for the intercom on his desk. In less than ten seconds one of his clerks appeared. "Please bring me all the files we have on Alex and Betsy Morton." Just as the clerk turned to leave, Wexler stopped her and said, "And also Azayiz and Saima Dansinghani."

"Alex, I'm not trained to protect you in this situation. You need a criminal lawyer." The clerk knocked but did not wait for an answer. She walked in with a pile of files up to her chin and put them on the table Wexler had just cleared for that purpose. She nodded to Wexler and walked out of the office. Wexler stood and closed the door once more. Wexler sorted through the stack and extracted those folders that had anything to do with scientific studies including all lab notes that he had received from Azi. "Take these files. I have no advice on what you should do with them but you can figure that one out. If the grand jury requests that I turn over files to them, I will honestly respond that I don't have files germane to their inquiry. Be careful, some of these contain Azi's confidential lab notes. How is Azi?"

"Azi's in California at UC-Berkley Medical Center."

Wexler broke in. "He's absented the jurisdiction! That's something for you to consider, Alex. In the meantime, as I said, you need a criminal defense lawyer. I suggest Hugh Fawbush. He comes off as folksy but don't let that fool you. He's as sharp as Zorro's sword and can parry with the best of them. Here's his telephone number. You're going to have to deal with Marty on your hospital privileges. I can't help you there, given my position on the hospital board."

"He already called. I haven't called him back yet. Alex gathered his files. Thanks, David, you've been a great help and a great friend. We'll stay in touch."

On the way home he stopped for a hamburger through the express line at Steak 'n Shake. After finishing the last of the French fries, he wiped the catsup from his fingers on his records and dumped them in the garbage bin behind the restaurant.

Alex met with Hugh Fawbush a few days later. Fawbush sported a walrus mustache of brown and gray that balanced curly, some would say unruly, brown hair that cascaded down his forehead. He wore a sport coat over a shirt with an open collar. His lapel pin was Mick Jagger's red lips. He spoke with a casual style, almost a drawl. Alex had heard that before, during his stint at MD Anderson.

Fawbush said, "I've had time to talk to our friend David and to look at your case, sir. The grand jury likes to keep secrets, but I have been able to tickle a few keys. Someone named Dr. Patterson tipped off the Marion County Prosecutor about where he could discover incriminating material. The grand jury assigned two detectives to investigate. They issued those invitations to testify. So, that's where we are now.

"Prosecutor Baratz will try this himself. Count on leaks and intense media attention. He'll try to nail you, and then you'll have a chance to elect him as your mayor in the fall.

"I'm going to request a week's delay for your testimony so we'll have time to think about and discuss this matter. I will recommend that you say nothing to the grand jury. You should exercise your Fifth Amendment rights, but that's a decision we will make together. I'm going to let Baratz know that I have been retained. His office won't bother you anymore. My preliminary judgment is that the grand jury will indict you for reckless homicide. At that point the case will be as pesky as a boll weevil.

"We don't make promises in this office, but we will make your case as best we can. We will emphasize that your spouse was a voluntary participant in this escapade and, in fact, demanded to be included. Your prior irrational conduct at the hospital is well-documented and will add to our burden. We'll try to keep past misadventures out of the record. Dr. Colson will probably give you a courtesy call to let you know your privileges have been suspended again. No doubt the Indiana Medical Licensing Board is looking at license revocation proceedings. When either event occurs, notify me right away.

"I have had tougher cases. Maybe we can achieve suspended jail time, probation, and community service. On the other hand, given your reputation for intelligence and creativity, Baratz may attach a motive and whack you with murder one. Did your wife carry a lot of life insurance? Either way, you'll be lower than a snake's belly in Indiana, maybe forever."

Alex returned the call to Colson as soon as he returned to the lab. "Marty, it's Alex."

"Alex, I've got no selection in this matter. We've sent you a letter suspending your privileges pending the outcome of the grand jury investigation. Our PR folks have been holding off the *Indianapolis Star,* but I know they intend to inflict severe damage on you and me. You'll be portrayed as a villain. I would cancel your mother's newspaper subscription if I were you."

"Thanks Marty. I have already spoken to my mom and dad and Betsy's mom and dad."

******

A week later Alex called the Jester. "Ralph, I need you to do me a big favor."

"Of course, Alex. How may I help you?"

"I'm going to pick you up at your home tomorrow afternoon at 2:00. I'd rather not come by the hospital."

"Sure, Alex."

At precisely 2 p.m. Alex pulled the blue Corvette into the Jester's driveway and bade him get in. Mendel curled up between Alex and the Jester with a paw on the Jester's leg. The Jester reached into his pocket and handed Mendel a peanut butter cracker. He leaned back and lit a cigarette.

"Ralph, thank you for helping me. After I drop myself off, I want you to take this car to the Wolfsonian Museum on Keystone Avenue and hand the letter I left in the console to Bud."

Alex drove north on U.S. 65 until he reached the third Lebanon exit. He headed west. Within fifteen minutes they saw nothing but corn and barley. Alex turned right on a dirt road. The blue 'Vette bounced along for three miles before Alex skidded to a stop in a gravel lot adjoining what aviators refer to as a "grass strip."

Alex opened the door and Mendel hopped out and waited while Alex retrieved a valise from the trunk of the car. He took three steps toward the gate, returned, clasped the Jester on the shoulder, and said, "Ralph, you are a great friend and I am fortunate to have a few friends like you, but there is nothing for me here now but bad memories." He turned back to the gate. He and Mendel disappeared into the waiting twin-engine turboprop that had paused for them as it taxied down the field.

The Jester lit another cigarette while he stared into the sky until even his imagination could no longer discern the aircraft. It was headed due south and with it the Jester's dreams of immortality.

PART THREE
ZABARDAST

CHAPTER THIRTY-SIX

"How's our patient?" Brenda quizzed Arvelia, the nurse practitioner from At Home Health Services who was assigned to weekend duty at Doc's home.

"He never complains, but he continues to require assistance with mobility and basic health requirements. His spirit is good, and his mind is active. Here, look at this crossword puzzle from the *New York Times* completely filled in. I walked him down to the pond around 10:00. It took about a half hour. He said he could move faster, but he wanted to enjoy the morning. I bet!"

Brenda set the grocery bag on the counter, and she and Dede began preparations for lunch. Brenda tossed a chicken salad while Dede combined strawberries, oranges, and fresh-cut pineapple.

"Dede, it's after 11 o'clock. I suggest you run down to the pond and help Papa up the path. I know it's early, but it's been taking longer for Papa. Besides, I could use a little extra time with Dad, er, Papa, to discuss plans for his 85th birthday party."

"Mary called from the office and left these messages that came in this morning. Papa can tend to them after lunch. After a year of retirement, he is still asked for advice almost every day, and he always returns his calls. He says it's his duty, but I know he loves to stay connected."

Dede replied on her way out the door, "That fits my plans. I need some time to discuss my basic anatomy exam coming up this Thursday, and I have to be back at school this afternoon."

Dede skipped down the path. This little bit of exercise felt refreshing. Hobbies and outside interests, including regular exercise, were losing the battle for time and attention to the demands of first-year medical school.

At the path's edge, Dede glanced across the bridge for a first glimpse of her grandfather relaxing on his bench.

He wasn't there.

"Papa."

Dede quickened her pace. "Papa," she said, practically choking. She found him half-folded on the grass at the base of the bench. A blue jay was pecking at the cuff of his pants.

******

The funeral was set for 11 a.m. at Tabernacle Presbyterian Church, known by all as Tab. By 10:30 there were no seats left in the sanctuary, including the 100 folding chairs placed along the back wall and in the aisles, a gross violation of Indianapolis fire code. Nobody cared. Mourners continued to file through the two church entrances well past 11:00. Most of them would have to be satisfied with watching from the lobby over the church audio-video system.

At 11:30 the Reverend Harris approached the pulpit. "Please rise." Half of the assemblage was already on its feet. The Tab choir sang "Amazing Grace" as the remainder of the congregation stood and added their voices. The hymn came to its resounding end with the repetition of the first stanza:

"Amazing Grace,
How sweet the sound
That saved a wretch like me.
I once was lost but now am found,
Was blind, but now I see.
Was blind, but now I see."

The Reverend Harris signaled for everyone to be seated. He began. "We are gathered today to mourn the loss of a fellow congregant, family member, and friend. Our community grieves with us today. Milton Elias Adams was born on October 10, 1933. He was the third child of Harry and May Adams. Milton's oldest brother, Theodore, died before Milton was born, and his brother Henry passed in 2001. He also survived his wife, Janie, who left this earth more than twenty years ago.

"When Milton was a child, he excelled in chess. He was a Boy Scout, achieving the rank of Eagle Scout. He loved to play football and baseball in our TAB rec leagues. Later, he developed an interest in music and fishing. Milton attended Duke University, enrolling in pre-med courses and majoring in chemistry. There was never a question of his desire to serve his community as a physician, just like his father, whom he often accompanied on house calls. He graduated from the IU School of Medicine, and after his internship and a residency in pediatrics, established his office in 1967.

"Milton was a proud member here at Tab, although he did not attend often. In spite of this seeming contradiction, he had faith in God. He had a strong moral sense—a sense of fairness and justice.

"Milton Adams, known by most of us as Milty or Doc, practiced pediatrics for almost fifty years at Rosenbaum Children's Hospital and in his office, just blocks from where we sit today. He practiced even as Parkinson's slowly tightened its grip. With the able assistance of his nurse, Mary Kellogg, he labored on, even as his coordination began to fail. He finally succumbed to a cardiac arrest. The family has asked Mary to read from the Book of Job."

Mary stood at the reader's podium and began. She paused to wipe her eyes but could not continue. Brenda rushed to her side and after an embrace they recited the verses together:

Oh, that my words were written!
Oh, that they were inscribed in a book!
That they were engraved on a rock
With an iron pen and lead, forever!
For I know that my Redeemer lives.

And He shall stand at last on the earth;
And after my skin is destroyed, this I know,
That in my flesh I shall see God,
Whom I shall see for myself,
And my eyes shall behold, and not another
How my heart yearns within me.

They held hands as they returned to their seats.

The Reverend Harris began again. "The children Doc cared for number in the thousands. Many of those children brought him their children. His gentle touch and sound advice spanned three generations. He was an extraordinary clinician with uncanny diagnostic acumen. He was a gracious counselor who enjoyed sharing his knowledge with colleagues, who often sought his advice and mentorship on difficult cases, long after new medicines and new techniques had rendered many doctors his age into a fading irrelevancy.

Doc's granddaughter, Dede, who is proudly carrying on the Adams' legacy as a first-year medical student at Indiana University, mentioned that her Papa had fielded more than a dozen calls the week before his death. In 1987, Doc was honored with the Ballantine Humanitarian Award, a national recognition by the American Pediatric Society. Today we will hear from Dede and from colleague Martin Colson, former CEO of Rosenbaum Hospital. First, Dr. Colson."

Martin Colson found the blue suit he often used to wear to the hospital. He considered the "red power tie," but Teddi chose a subdued blue one for him. He hesitated before addressing the congregation. As a hospital administrator for many years, Colson was adept at public speaking, but he had never addressed an assemblage so crammed in that those who stood could not even shift their feet. The scene was further complicated by the grief on their faces.

Colson gathered himself and began, "Milty was my friend. One of my best friends. We worked together for half a century. We laughed together. He was gentle and caring with his patients—and *about* those patients. While other physicians refused to take non-paying patients, Milty declared his practice open to everyone, whether or not they could afford medical care. He was proud of a bill he fought tirelessly for in the Indiana state legislature that created the Catastrophic Illness Children's Relief Fund. This premiere program was the first of its kind in the United States that provided assistance to families struggling with the responsibilities of caring for and coping with a seriously ill child.

All those years when I served Rosenbaum, Milty was the glue who held the hospital together. He was willing to share his knowledge with professional colleagues and students. You already heard that there was no one better at diagnosis. As to the game of bridge, there was no one worse."

Colson paused, "He was a steady guy who was there for me with advice and assistance whenever I asked. That advice was requested on medical and humanitarian matters—not business. His wife, Janie, had told me a long time ago, 'When Milt entered medical school, he checked his business brains at the door.' Milty and I were on the phone just last week remembering old times, and now he's gone." Colson paused again, this time to compose himself.

"The world has lost a brilliant doctor and human being who was not only deeply loved by family, friends, and patients alike, but was greatly respected and admired by those of us in the medical profession. He was a man filled with enormous humanity, compassion, depth of feeling, and devotion to helping others." Colson shook his head and went to his seat.

Dede hugged Colson in passing and took her place at the podium. "My grandmother would have wanted me to say something today. She met Papa at a fraternity party when they were both undergraduates at Duke. Grandma wrote in her diary, 'From the minute I talked to him, I felt like I didn't need to ever talk to another person again.' Papa adored my grandmother. It was a cruel blow to lose her so many years ago. Papa lived in the same home at the end of Cherrywood Lane for more than fifty years. When they bought it, it was considered to be way out in the country. It seemed he and that house grew old together. Grandma and Papa loved that house. They enjoyed the five-acre back yard and the pond—Papa's precious pond. After grandma's death, Papa had to make a major adjustment. He became more absorbed in his practice and he spent more time playing bridge. Dr. Colson told you about that."

Dede waited for the laughter and began again. "Papa was a dedicated, caring, and exceptionally skilled physician—he loved being a doctor. He was a master of the art of medicine, not just the science of medicine.

Papa was always available to his patients, and he took patient calls, no matter the hour or if he was on vacation. He made house calls during the week in which he retired. Who makes house calls anymore? Grandma told me about Papa's first house call. He had just opened his office. The child had pneumonia and needed an antibiotic. Grandma said to Papa when he walked in about 9:00 that night, 'How nice it is to finally have some income.' Papa replied, 'I'm afraid I have some bad news about my fee. The family could not afford it and in fact, I went to the pharmacy and purchased the medicine I prescribed for the baby.' Such was the start of Papa's private practice career. He deeply valued each life, taking the time to know every patient as a person, and developed close personal relationships with them all. He was tolerant and non-judgmental and always did his best to alleviate illness or suffering, physical or emotional.

Papa was a gift to me. Speaking of gifts, I was about five years old when I had the chance to sleep over at Papa's house. When I arrived that evening, he gave me a special gift, a doctor's bag with all the tools of the doctor's trade, including a plastic hypodermic needle, a stethoscope, a little flashlight, and some small bandages and Band-Aids. I was very proud to pretend to be a doctor just like Papa, and I played with the toys all evening. Before I went to bed, I placed my bag right next to his in the front foyer. That night Papa had to make a house call. I remember it was a snowy day. It must have been a cold and snowy evening, as well. Papa arrived at the patient's home, opened his bag and pulled out my toy stethoscope. The next morning at breakfast he gently inquired, 'Dede have you seen my stethoscope? I said, "Well yes, Papa, the one that was in my doctor's bag didn't seem to work very well, so I traded you.' This year, on my first day of medical school, Papa gave me a real stethoscope."

Papa struggled with Parkinson's disease, which he fought with grace and toughness. He never gave in to it. He won that battle for dozens of years, until it finally contributed to his death. Papa touched and transformed thousands of lives. Please do something for me. If you are not already standing and if you were one of Papa's patients, please stand." Dede gasped at the breathtaking response.

"He was a true hero in every sense of the word. He was my hero. He was my Papa." Dede wiped her tears as she took her seat.

The Reverend Harris shared his final thoughts. "As you leave this sanctuary, remember goodness is measured not by years on earth but by deeds in those years. Vow to emulate this great man whose life we celebrate today. May God go with you." The Tab choir softly sang, "How Great Thou Art."

Then sings my soul, My Savior God, to Thee,
How great Thou art, How great Thou art.
Then sings my soul, My Savior God, to Thee,
How great Thou art, How great Thou art!

When Christ shall come with shout of acclamation,
And take me home, what joy shall fill my heart.
Then I shall bow in humble adoration,
And then proclaim: "My God, how great thou art!"

The Reverend Harris referred to his notes. "Pallbearers are Martin Colson, Bob Block, David Wexler, Margo Thompson, and Ralph Jessup. Honorary pallbearers are Doc's patients, who he often referred to as 'my perfect patients.'"

In the limousine on the way to the cemetery, Brenda said, "Dede, I am proud of you. Papa would have been proud too. Thank you."

Dede said in a hushed voice, "Mom, as I stood before that congregation, I knew they were all looking back at me, but I made contact with someone who stared deep into my soul. It was that old lady Papa and I saw years ago at Mrs. Morton's funeral—the one in the green dress and flowered hat. Thank God she ditched that ugly dress. The lady was crying again."

Brenda put her arm around Dede's shoulder. "Dede, that old woman in the flowered hat is your father."

CHAPTER THIRTY-SEVEN

Mother and daughter sat together on the floor in Doc's library surrounded by files, books, and assorted papers, evidence of a full and active career. Brenda had cleared her father's bookshelves and emptied on the floor the three large boxes of books and personal contents Mary had delivered from Doc's office.

"David Wexler assured me we have plenty of time to open Papa's estate. It's been only three weeks, so we don't really need to do this today, but I wanted to start cleaning out Papa's office. I'm glad you came over to help, Dede. It will give us time to talk.

"Let's put these books in piles. The medical textbooks and journals that you don't want, I'll donate to Rosenbaum. Let's gift the casual reading books to Teachers' Treasures. Did you ever read this one?" Brenda held up *The Last Angry Man*. "The title character is a doctor and a man of principle, a good man guided by a belief in basic human decency. Maybe Papa saw a little of himself in there.

Your grandmother loved scrapbooks. I'll keep these." Brenda caressed the pages. She caught the photographs falling out of the scrapbooks and reinserted each one with care. She said, "It's a wonder anyone knew what your grandfather looked like. He always had a camera in front of his face. Look Dede, there I am as a young girl with your grandparents. Look at those pigtails! And here they are on a Voyager Trip to Acapulco with Alex and Betsy. Dad didn't want to take more than a few days at a time away from his practice, so they joined the Voyager Travel Club. It flew members non-stop to vacation destinations throughout Mexico and the Caribbean at dirt-cheap prices. It worked because all Voyager offered was third class. They really packed them in. Your grandfather said he felt like an oarsman on a Viking ship."

"Mom, tell me about Alex and Betsy."

"I'll get to that when we have more time."

"Now, Mom!"

"Here are a couple of fat files of thank you's and newsy items about Papa's patients. Remember the Ginnis boy? He was a preemie. This picture shows him at 6 feet, 8 inches, playing forward for the Indiana Pacers."

"Right now, Mom!"

"Okay Dede, here are files we can look at together."

Brenda chose the folder labeled "Heaven-Sent Storage Bank." She rested on an elbow as she placed the first item between them. It was a letter to Alex Morton marked "personal and confidential."

Heaven-Sent Storage Bank
2600 S. Michigan Ave., Suite 1150
Chicago, IL 60612

March 17, 1979

Alex Morton, M.D.
12635 Broad Street
Carmel, IN 46032

Re: Alex Morton, M.D., Account No. S121640

Dear Dr. Morton:

We are pleased to inform you that your account has been established successfully. We have preserved three sperm deposits established by you on March 15, 1979.

We acknowledge your payment of $485 as paid in full for collection and cryo-storage service for one year from the date of your deposit.

We appreciate your confidence in our company.

Yours very truly,

Yoko Watanabi

Yoko Watanabi, Chief Technical Officer
cc: Milton Adams, M.D.

The next letter was a notice that the second year's fee was due. Dede flipped to the third letter.

Heaven-Sent Storage Bank
2600 S. Michigan Ave., Suite 1150
Chicago, IL 60612

March 15, 1993

Alex Morton, M.D.
12635 Broad Street
Carmel, IN 46032

Registered Mail
Return Receipt Requested

Re: Alex Morton, M.D.
Account No. S121640
Outstanding Balance $350

Dear Dr. Morton:

Pursuant to Ill. Statute 8654, you are hereby notified that you have thirty days in which to bring your account current. If we do not hear from you by May 1, 1993, we will terminate the account referenced above and dispose of the contents of your deposit in our sperm bank.

Please contact the undersigned as soon as possible to rectify this situation.

Yours very truly,

Yoko Watanabi

Yoko Watanabi,
Chief Technical Officer
cc: Milton Adams, M.D.

"Here's a letter from Papa."

Milton Adams, M.D.
120 Cherrywood Lane
Indianapolis, IN 46260

March 22, 1993

Yoko Watanabi
Heaven-Sent Sperm Bank
2600 S. Michigan Ave., Suite 1150
Chicago, IL 60612

Re: Alex Morton, M.D.
Account No. S121640

Dear Ms. Watanabi:

Enclosed please find our check in the sum of $350, payment in full on the above listed account.

By the authority vested in me by the Power of Attorney of April 15, 1979, a copy of which is attached hereto, please be advised that the office of Dr. Ward Yosso will contact you on or before April 15, 1993 to coordinate the delivery of sperm in this account suitable for artificial insemination.

We would be pleased to honor any reasonable expenses incurred in complying with this request.

Yours very truly,

Milton Adams, M.D.

cc: Ward Yosso, M.D.
David Wexler, J.D.

Dede placed the letters back in the file. Brenda closed the file and turned to her daughter with tears in her eyes. "We lost your father to testicular cancer when you were two years old. You know that, but you don't know that he was not your biological father. The radiation treatment he endured rendered him sterile. We hoped your father would survive for much longer and we wanted a little girl just like you to love. Your father did love you dearly. We asked Papa for advice and he referred me to Dr. Yosso. While all of this was going on, Papa was notified of the delinquency in Alex's account. Papa brought the account current and directed that Alex's deposits be delivered to Dr. Yosso, who performed the artificial insemination."

"You mean I started out swirling in Dr. Yosso's petri dish?"

"Yes, and look at you now—brilliant and gorgeous. Papa could not have chosen a better donor."

"Mom, didn't he murder his wife?"

Dede deftly turned back to the family scrapbook, extracted the photo of the Mortons, and the Adams and placed it in her purse.

"Where is Alex? I want to speak to him. I want to know him."

"I have no idea where he is. Papa may have known. We can look through the rest of his papers, but I doubt if Papa would have left any clues."

"I'll find him."

CHAPTER THIRTY-EIGHT

"Which of these dresses should I wear?" Dede thought, it's not every day that the deans of the medical profession invite a brand-new graduate to dinner.

Brenda made her choice. She said to herself, "I'll wear the blue one. It's professional yet feminine. There is still some life left in those old codgers."

Dede was flattered when Marty Colson had called and invited her on behalf of Doc's buddies, Ralph Jessup, David Wexler, and Margo Thompson. Dede was enjoying her day, first graduation and now getting ready for dinner and a chance to learn more about her grandfather from his closest friends.

The doorbell rang and Brenda yelled down the hall, "Dede, it's for you."

A boy in clean white overalls and a white cap sporting a logo of a laughing two-legged red wolf handed Dede a box the size of a paperback book. It rattled and clanged when she shook it. The delivery boy implored her to open the box. She did and extracted a set of keys. He then pointed to the driveway. Dede screamed with delight. It was a gleaming classic powder blue Corvette. She remembered her grandfather reminiscing about Alex's car and how it roared. She looked back in the box and read the note.

"Dede,
Congratulations on graduation from medical school.
Love, Alex"

Dede stopped the delivery boy as he proceeded to the automobile that had been dispatched for his return and asked, "Where has this Corvette been for 40 years?"

"We have displayed this magnificent sports car at the Wolfsonian Museum on Keystone Avenue for many years longer than I have been employed," said the teen. "I understand from the Wolf family that the storage fee had been paid in advance and that the instructions were to hold the car pending further notice. A couple of years ago, the explicit direction was to deliver the 'Vette on the day of your graduation from medical school, with the proviso that if you did not graduate by 2020, the Wolfsonian was entitled to keep the car as part of its own collection. I was kinda hoping you wouldn't graduate in time. I forgot to mention that the title will be mailed to you within the next few days. Enjoy! Can you operate a stick shift? It's a kick to drive."

At 6:00 that evening Colson picked up Dede in a limousine and took her to his favorite restaurant, Vida, an adventure in inventive dining with a price to match. They were escorted to a private room. Waiting for them were Ralph Jessup, David Wexler, and Margo Thompson. Jessup, who after a long career, finally embraced his nickname, "the Jester," as it was now offered with a warm familiarity, particularly by Thompson. They were quite close. Hospital chatter referred to them as an "item." He was wheelchair-bound. Dede bent to hold his hand and said, "Papa talked about you all the time." Thompson embraced Dede like a sister. She said, "I loved your grandfather. He was always there for me and I will always be there for you."

Over cocktails, talk turned to hospital tales—tall and otherwise. Marty said, "Well, finally we reconfigured that old lab space on the sixth floor, particularly the area behind the radioactive door. It's a children's lounge. I'll be darned if the money for those improvements wasn't provided by the same family that donated the funds to renovate the hospital years ago, including the establishment of the Institute on Aging. It was Alex's brother-in-law, Liam Howell, who made the donation in honor of his sister, Betsy Howell Morton."

The Jester piped up, "You know, nobody knew this at the time, but there was nothing radioactive behind that radioactive door. It was just a super private area. I know because I had been in there once or twice."

Marty answered, "Well, the irony here is that after a couple of years, when we gave up waiting for Alex to return, I called the hazmat company we used to dispose of our hospital waste. I forget its name now. They came out in space suits and sealed the cylindrical containers used to freeze tissues and cell samples, everything from nematodes to Rhesus monkeys, and carted them off to a hazardous waste dump out by the old junkyard, Wrecks Inc. By now they'd be buried under 100 feet of truly radioactive material."

The Jester said, "I bet you $1,000 bucks you could still bring those nematodes back to life."

Colson said, "Don't think so, Jester. They may have been in those tanks more than forty years. I'll tell you a bigger mystery. You know that beautiful painting in Alex's private office?"

The Jester said, "You mean the Monet? Everyone in the hospital talked about that."

"Yes, it was a Monet, and I'm told a painting worth millions. Well, it disappeared about the same time Alex went on the lam. I admitted investigators to that office two weeks later. The place was a mess, with files all over the floor. The cops had no idea the Monet was missing, and I didn't offer it. Over the couch was that poster of Raquel Welch that Alex used to illustrate his lectures."

Cocktails arrived and Colson proposed a toast, "To the newest member of the medical profession, Dr. Dede Paller."

"Actually, it's Dede Morton. With my mother's encouragement I am going to formally change my name to honor my father." It was no secret that Dede was Alex's biological daughter. Dede had been proud to share that information with anyone and everyone as soon as she understood what it meant and how it came about.

A voice from the door said, "Huzzah! Somebody hand me a glass of champagne. I'll drink to that." Everyone looked up. It was Azi.

Dede said, "Azi, I thought I saw you at my graduation. I hoped it was you. You were sitting way in the back."

"Yes, Dede, I wouldn't miss it. Alex and Doc were my family. You are, too."

Dede tried to hide her astonishment. According to her calculation, Azi would be about seventy, yet he bore no sign of the last four decades. Barely a wrinkle. His hair was the same jet black as the photographs she remembered on her Papa's wall at home. She thought, "But of course!"

"Azi, California has treated you very well, and I am so flattered that you would come across the continent to congratulate me on this special day." They embraced as Dede wiped the tears from her eyes. She took her handkerchief and wiped a couple of tears from Azi's eyes as well.

The Jester looked up at Azi from his wheelchair. "You've gained weight, Azi, and it looks good on you. You used to be as skinny as a pogo stick. Here, have a gummy bear."

Colson leaned back in his chair and said, "Do you remember old Yosso, the obstetrician that they used to call 'Goldfinger?' The week he disappeared they found his car in our parking lot and so I was questioned by the police. For a time, they suspected his nurse of doing away with him in a fit of jealous rage. Apparently, he was carrying on with patients, nurses, and just about anything that wore a skirt and didn't oink. He was a friend of Teddi's and mine as well as your grandfather. But I guess nobody knew of his dalliances, or if they did, kept it quiet. I like to think maybe he's rolling in the feathers somewhere with a couple of nurses, but I suspect the worst because if he were alive today, Dede, he would be here. After all, he had something to do with your birth."

Margo changed the subject. "Speaking of missing persons, has anybody ever heard from Alex?"

Dede addressed everyone. "I spent all last summer and most of my savings looking for him. There were clues and maybe I came close, but I'll never know. When Jimmy Higgins died in August, I came home knowing for certain that Alex would be at the funeral in the unattractive green dress with the polka-dot shoes or one of his other disguises. He was not, or at least I couldn't spot him. Alex loved that boy. I did run into Hilary Stout, you know, nurse Stout in Alex's office. I hadn't met her, but mom pointed her out to me. She had to be one of the tallest women in the room and she had a commanding presence. She was happy to meet me. When I asked her about Alex, she turned polite and was gone the minute I turned my head. I went back on the trail for the last few weeks before school. I mean, how difficult can it be to find a man and a dog?" Azi busied himself folding and refolding his napkin.

Margo interrupted, "Wait a minute, Dede. That dog would only live about twelve years."

Dede replied, "That's most dogs, but not Mendel. Doc told me that Mendel was destined to live at least a half a century. You know, the more I thought about Hilary Stout, the more I believed she held clues to Alex. But then, school intervened and here we are. I did determine she no longer resides in Indiana."

Azi was quiet. Dede turned to him and said, "How is Saima? Did Faraz ever have a brother or a sister?"

"Unfortunately, no. The protocol in which Saima had been on for many years precluded her from becoming pregnant. But thanks for asking about Faraz. He lives in Wisconsin and has a career and a family of his own. We are quite proud."

When the main course was completed, Dede raised her glass and said, "Let's toast to my grandfather, Doc, whose influence inspired us to live up to his ideals. I loved my grandfather, and I know you all did as well. To Doc!" In unison, all repeated, "to Doc."

David Wexler had long since retired, although he retained a few clients who were special to him, including Marty Colson. Now devoted to his golf game at least four days a week, he bragged to his friends that if it were a sunny day, he'd be at the golf course, and if it were a rainy day, he'd be at the racetrack. Wexler's long shaggy brown hair had turned to an exquisite silver. He turned to Dede and apologized. "Dede, about Alex, perhaps I should have given you some clues, but as a lawyer who has sworn to maintain confidences, which I did through-out my career, I declined to provide direction. Let me be clear. I never knew exactly where he was, but I did hear from him from time to time. He knew he could trust me and I didn't let him down. After Alex disappeared and a grand jury indicted him on reckless homicide, throughout my career, try as I might, I could never quash those charges. That indictment is still in effect. There will always be an outstanding warrant. Consequently, he has remained a fugitive."

Dede looked at Wexler, "David, like I said, I did try to find him all summer. I thought maybe I had found him when I learned of a saint of a man who was healing patients at a remote outpost called 'Eldoret' in Kenya's Great Rift Valley. Speaking of Mendel, there was an article in the "EastAfrican" about this doctor who was grieving over the loss of his dog, who had been dragged away by a cheetah. By the time I got there, all was gone. No doctor, no dog, and no cheetah. Was it Alex? Nurses said the doctor was the right height, but he was bald. They had no photographs. According to the article, the doctor's name was Kevin, Kevin Moore. Alex's father was named Kevin Morton."

The Jester twirled his wheelchair to face Dede. "What was the dog's name?"

Dede nodded. "It was Mendel."

"I flew to Costa Rica when I saw a photograph in the magazine, "Surfs Up" of surfers with remarkable balance. He had blond hair but the blue eyes were unmistakable. It was Alex. By the time I got to the beach in Jacó, he had moved on. Where he went, I do not know. Maybe he was running from someone more sinister than I, or maybe he was just running. The other guy in the photograph, a Tico named Marco, said a man with a mustache named Louis asked him a bunch of questions about Alex. That would have been Betsy's brother. I can tell you Alex left Jacó in mid-August for a small airport 50 kilometers south, where he boarded a charter flight to who knows where. I have checked with authorities, federal, state, and Interpol. He is traveling on fake identification documents, because nothing shows up for Alex Morton or for Kevin Moore.

"I investigated the widow, Mrs. Morton, Alex's mother, whose funeral I attended when I was a teenager. She died at 106. She had been taking the therapy that Alex created and which had apparently killed Betsy. My guess is that Mrs. Morton ran out of friends and zest for life and chose not to continue to drink from the fountain of youth. I learned from my old boyfriend that there were a number of discarded packages around her house from Mexico City marked "artichokes." I followed that lead and contacted the manager of the artichoke company, who informed me that someone had purchased the artichokes with instructions to deliver them to an old building a few miles from the factory. Apparently, Alex drained the jars and refilled them with what people told me he called 'el jugo.' I guess he had figured out how to make his elixir in an injectable form. Of course, the warehouse had been abandoned.

"I am teary-eyed when I think of Alex. His love affair with Betsy was as deep a love as any two people could share, and the emotional stress of losing her the way he did must have torn him to tatters. I hope he has fallen in love again."

Azi raised his glass. "Let's toast an extraordinary man, brilliant beyond any other and courageous beyond measure, a man who jeopardized a career for the sake of a young boy, a man who loved beyond boundaries and who shared that love with all of us, but mostly with his precious Betsy. May he allow us to find him once again and return that love, but if he chooses to wander this world alone, let him do so with the happiness he so richly deserves.

"Zabardast!"

ACKNOWLEDGMENTS

It is an honor to be among the titles published by IBJ Book Publishing Company. Thank you Jodi Belcher, Manager, and team for your work, including the brilliant cover design.

Thanks to Julia Whitehead, whose ideas animated some of my characters and to copy editor Tawn Parent who provided many hours of assistance in converting my manuscript into readable text. I appreciate her careful attention to detail and patience in putting up with my stream of additions and revisions.

A note of appreciation goes to: Jim Voyles, Bill Vincent, Mercy Obeime, Eddie Yosowitz, Eric Prystowsky, Jon Fisch, Tom Harton, AJ Correale, Christopher Leaman, David Zipes, David Coats, Lawrence Einhorn, Sharon Wellbrook, Michael Sherman, Scott Newman, Faraz Abbasi, Michael Prystowsky, and Dan Simon.

I gratefully acknowledge the valuable research, insightful observation and cheerful support of my executive assistant, Susan Roederer.

Thank you, Janie Maurer, my wife, who is always my collaborator and helpful critic.

ABOUT THE AUTHOR

Michael S. "Mickey" Maurer lives in Carmel, Indiana, with his wife, Janie. The Maurers have three children and nine grandchildren. Contact Maurer at mmaurer@ibj.com.